BEAU SPECS

Adolescent, confused and often broke, 'Specs' is back in an enthralling sequel to 'Specs' War'.

Cecil 'Specs' Kensal is now a teenager in the early 1950s. His dad has suddenly reappeared, apparently from Down Under, which is a bit of a problem, seeing as Specs' Mam and Uncle Sid have been sharing a bed for years now. More to the point, what to do about Specs? No longer a child, not yet an adult, Specs hungers for adventures. If only he was a bit older, if only he had enough money for his fare, if only he had a passport—he'd join the Foreign Legion. 'Beau Specs' sounds pretty good, doesn't it? ...

BEAU SPECS

BEAU SPECS

by

Sara Fraser

Magna Large Print Books
Long Preston, North Yorkshire,
England.

British Library Cataloguing in Publication Data.

Fraser, Sara
Beau Specs.

A catalogue record for this book is available from the British Library

ISBN 1-7505-1381-0

First published in Great Britain by Severn House Publishers Ltd., 1998

Published in Large Print 1999 by arrangement with Severn House Publishers Ltd.

Magna Large Print is an imprint of
Library Magna Books Ltd.
Printed and bound in Great Britain by
T.J. International Ltd., Cornwall, PL28 8RW.

Introduction

Here's 'Specs' Kensal again. Now a young teenager in the early 1950s. No longer a child. Not yet an adult. Specs hungers for the adventures that he is convinced are waiting for him beyond the confines of his Midlands home town. If only he was a bit older. If only he had enough money for his fare. If only he had a passport ... He'd join the Foreign Legion.

Meanwhile, life goes on ... And for poor, baffled frustrated Specs, what a life it is!

One

I hate my job, you know. Me Mam found it for me when I left school last year. She says that in years to come I'll thank her for doing it. She says that I'll have a job for life on the 'Gas'.

But I don't want to be on the Gas. I want to be like Beau Geste and call meself 'Beau' Specs and join the Foreign Legion and have lots of adventures. I've read the book and seen the film hundreds of times, you know. It's brilliant! My favourite bit is where they find Fort Zinderneuf full of dead men.

I'm going to join the Foreign Legion as soon as I've saved enough money to go to France. I'm saving for a passport as well because you have to have a passport to travel with, don't you. Unless you're in the Forces, or the Merchant Navy. That must be good to sail around the world like that. I like to read about travelling, but my Mam goes mad when she catches me reading books about travelling, or about the Foreign Legion. She says that I'm a wicked, ungrateful young bastard to want to leave a good home and the Mother who's worked herself to death to bring me up. She says I ought to be happy to stay with her and look after her when she gets old. She's always nagging at me though, so how can I be happy to stay with her when she's doing that all the time?

I hate living at home. It was bad enough when there was just me Mam and Uncle Sid, Uncle Harold and Hilda, Granny Smith and me and me sister Virgy living here, but now me Dad's come back it's terrible.

I couldn't believe it when he come back last week. He run away from us when I was still a babby, and Virgy has always told me that it was my fault he run away in the first place. She says that when I was born he took one look at me and went out of the door and never come back. She says he couldn't stand the sight of me because I was so ugly. She's a horrible cow, our Virgy is. Two years older than me, a face full of spots, lanky and skinny and ginger-haired. Compared to her looks I'm a film star, even with me glasses on.

Anyway, me Dad came back last week.

Late on Tuesday night, it was, and there was a knock at the back door, and our Virgy goes to the door and there's a scruffy little bloke with glasses standing there wearing a dirty old mac, and on his head he's got one of them Australian hats with corks dangling down all round it.

'Who're you? What d'you want?' our Virgy asks him.

'Is it really you, Virginia?' His voice sounded all strange and wavery.

'Well, it was when I got up this morning,' she says, all stroppy.

'I'm your Dad,' he tells her.

'What?'

'I'm your Dad.'

'MAAAMMMM!' She slams the door and starts screaming up the stairs. Because me Mam and Uncle Sid are having a early night.

At their age! Disgusting, aren't it!

'MAAAMMMM, there's a bloke down here who says he's me Dad!'

'WHAT?' Me Mam come downstairs like a rocket with only her nightie on and she rushes to the door.

'What the bleedin' hell am you doing here?' she shouts at the bloke.

'Effie, darlint, it's good to see you.' The

bloke holds his arms out.

'Well, it aren't good to see you, Horace Kensal! So you can just sod off back to where you've been for the last fifteen years.'

'I was at the war, Effie.'

'And where do you think the rest of us was, you rotten bugger? And the war ended bloody years and years ago, so where have you been 'til now?'

'I've been overseas, Effie.'

'Then you should have stayed there.'

'Bloody hell, Effie, this aren't much of a welcome home, is it,' me Dad grumbles, sounding all hard done by.

'It's all the bloody welcome you're going to get, so just sod off!'

'Oh, you don't really mean that, darlint. I know that you're pleased to see me really,' he tells her.

'Specs,' she tells me, 'go upstairs and fetch Uncle Sid down here.' Then she smiles all nasty at me Dad. 'My man 'ull soon show you the way down the road, my buck!'

When I get upstairs I can't see Uncle Sid at first. Then I spot his foot poking out from under the bed.

'Sid, me Mam wants you downstairs.'

I don't call him Uncle now that I'm left school and working. He's not me uncle anyway.

He don't answer me. So I say again:

'Sid, me Mam wants you downstairs. Me Dad's come home and me Mam wants you to throw him out.'

He still don't answer, so then I grab his foot, and he yells, 'Ohhh God! Tell your Dad it's all her fault. She caught me in her web like a spider snares a fly.'

'You're scared of him, aren't you? You're scared of me Dad.' I can't help rubbing it into him, because of all the tall stories he used to tell me when I was a nipper, about how brave and tough he was, and all the fighting and adventures he'd had, and all the medals he'd won. And I used to believe him! That's what gets me now. I used to believe all his bullshit.

He looked out from under the bed then.

'Scared!' he said all fierce. 'You dare to call Sidney Tompkin scared? Let me tell you, Sidney Tompkin is scared of no man. I'm only scared of what I might do if I come face to face with him. If the blood goes to me head I'll end up ripping him limb from limb.'

'I don't know about that, Sid. He's a big bloke.'

I've already seen that me Dad looks like a real weed, but I like teasing Sid.

'Ohhhh God!' Sid moans.

'I'll tell you what, Sid, he looks like a nutter to me. He's got funny staring eyes and he keeps on waving an axe around.'

'Ohhhhh God!' Sid slumps down as if he's fainted.

'Are you coming down, or what?'

'In a minute. I'll come down in a minute,' Sid says, all faint-like.

But the funny thing is that when I go back downstairs me Dad is sitting at the table and me Mam is in the kitchen making a cup of tea and sandwiches for him.

Virgy is sitting listening to me Dad telling her that he's been in Australia ever since the war ended.

'I had a big sheep ranch in the outback, down along the Yarra River. Covered about eighteen thousand square miles, it did.'

Then he tells me, 'It's good to see you again, Cecil.'

I hate that name! That's why I don't tell anybody what it is. I'm glad that everybody calls me Specs, because of me glasses.

'Nobody calls me Cecil.' I've got the hump against him straight away. 'They call me Specs.'

He looks all snotty. 'Cecil was my own dear old Dad's name, and that's why I give it to you, and that's what I'll call you whether you likes it or not.'

I go into the kitchen and ask me Mam, 'Is he really me Dad?'

'Oh yes. He's your Dad alright.'

It's funny how happy she's looking. She's humming to herself while she's spreading the fish-paste onto the bread and marge.

'Why are you making this for him? You always said that you hated him.'

She blushed then, and giggled all girlish-like. 'We all say things that we don't really mean. Go and tell him that I'm just waiting for the kettle to boil.'

I can't take this in, you know. She's always carried on about me Dad, and every time I asked her about him, she told me to shurrup and mind me own business. And every time I've done something to make her mad at me, she's always called me all the names under the sun and told me that I was just like that no-good bastard of a Dad of mine. And now he's come back she's all pleased and acting funny. I can't take it in.

'Don't stand there gawping at me, you gormless young sod. Go and tell your Dad what I said.' She lost her rag then and started skreeking at me, so I did what she wanted.

'Who's looking after your ranch now, Dad?' Virgy was all impressed, you could see that, her eyes all big and starry.

'I've sold it, darlint.' He looked ever so smug. 'Sold it for a fortune, I have. Your old Dad is a rich man, Virginia. A very rich man.'

Well, he don't look very rich to me, with his National Health teeth and glasses, and his trouser bottoms all frayed, and his shirt collar all dirty.

'Have you come back home for good, then?' Virgy wanted to know.

I'm seeing now that she's the spitting image of our Dad. They're both ugly!

I'm glad I don't look like them.

'That's right, darlint. I'm back in dear old Blighty for good. As soon as I can get my money transferred from Australia I'm going to buy a big house, and a car, and have a television in every room.'

'A television! In every room! Ohhh Dad!' Virgy squealed and clapped her hands like a little kid.

There's only one television in our street, and that's the one that the Jones-Evanses have got. They live in the big posh house at the top of the street. Idris and Sybil, their names are. A right pair of stuck-up prats they are as well. Aubrey, their son, is the same age as me, and he's a real Mammy's darling. None of the people round here like him.

I go and watch the television sometimes in Curry's shop window down the town. The only trouble is that you can't hear the sound so it's hard to know what's going on. And then when it rains there's no shelter so you get soaked.

Well, me Dad scoffs the grub like he's starving, and makes ever such a racket when he's eating and drinking. Then we sit there for hours listening to him bragging, and me Mam is being ever so nice to him, in fact the more he talks about how rich he is the nicer she gets.

Sid don't show his face at all.

What I can't understand is that Australia is supposed to be very hot with sunshine all the time, and me Dad is all white and pasty. So I ask him, 'Why aren't you all brown? I thought the sun always shone in Australia.'

He looks at me as if I'm mad. 'I'm a Bwana, Cecil. Bwanas don't go out into the sun. Bwanas stays in the shade.'

'Of course they does.' Me Mam nods all wisely. 'Any fool knows that.'

I'll tell you what I'm beginning to think. I'm beginning to think that me Dad is like me Uncle Sid. Full of bullshit! Because I read a lot of books and I know that Bwanas comes from Africa, not Australia.

Then me Mam asks him, 'Have you got anywhere to stay yet, Horace?'

And me Dad says, 'No, darlint. I came straight here as soon as I got off the boat. All me luggage is still on the High Seas on the boat that was following mine. I had to send it like that because there wasn't any room for it on the boat I come on. I've got just too much luggage, you see, darlint. Boxes and boxes and boxes of the stuff.'

'Well, you can stay here if you like,

Horace. Just until you buys your big house, of course,' me Mam tells him.

I can't take this in. Where's he going to sleep? Uncle Harold and Hilda have got the attic. Me Mam and Uncle Sid are in the front bedroom, Virgy is in the back bedroom and I've got a camp-bed in the front room. That just leaves this room, and there's only a table and some chairs and a bit of matting in front of the firegrate.

'You can have Specs's bed in the front room,' she says as calm as you like.

'Where am I going to sleep?' I ask her.

'You can sleep on the couch in the front room,' she tells me, 'and then tomorrow we'll make other arrangements.'

Before I can say anything me Mam starts screeching at me. 'Don't pull your face about like that, you ungrateful young bugger! I'se worked meself to death to bring you up. You should be happy to let your Dad have your bed now he's come all this way to see you. Look how pleased Virgy is to see her Dad back.'

Well, Virgy might be pleased, but it's not her bed he's taking, is it. I don't think much of this for a game of soldiers ...

Two

I'm mating Georgie Snood this week. He's the Gas Fitter that I have to work with most of the time. You see, what happens is that the Gas Fitters gets given jobs and then if they needs a Mate on the job one of us lads is sent to work with them. But some of the Fitters have a Mate with them all the time. They're training the Mates to be Gas Fitters. None of the Fitters wants me for a Mate, you know. They says I'm living in a Dream World. But I don't care. I don't want none of them for a Mate neither. Least of all Georgie Snood.

I don't like Georgie Snood. He don't like me neither. He says that I'm not a good Mate because I don't take no interest in the job. But how can I be interested when I don't want to do it? I want to join the Foreign Legion and have adventures, not go around fitting gas ovens and screwing pipes. Georgie Snood keeps on staring at me all sad and sorrowful, and shaking his head and saying, 'You're not Gas Fitter material, you're not. You'll never make a Gas Fitter as long as you've got a'nole in your arse.'

That's all he keeps on saying, all the time. Do you know I go to sleep some nights and dream I can hear him saying ... 'You're not Gas Fitter material, you're not. You'll never make a Gas Fitter as long as you've got a'nole in your arse.'

And then when I pass him the tools he'll swear and chuck them at me.

'I never asked for this, you yampy-yedded young bleeder! You're not Gas Fitter material, you're not.'

I know I'm not!

There's one kid I was at school with who's gone into the army as a boy soldier. When I see him come home on leave he don't half look good in his uniform. All the girls like him, because he can tell them about the adventures he's having. Last time he was home he told me that he's got more girlfriends than he knows what to do with.

I wish he'd give one of them to me.

I haven't got a girlfriend, you know. There's one girl that I really like, her name's Glenda Shortway, she works in the Building Society Office down town. She's got long blonde hair tied in a ponytail, and she's really pretty. Me and Johnny Merry were at the Memorial Hall dance a few weeks ago, and she was there as well. I wanted to ask her to dance with me, but I was too scared to. She was with some other girls, and I thought that they would all start taking the mickey if they saw how much I liked her.

The trouble is I'm not very good looking because I wear glasses, and me hair sticks up behind, so I have to use lots of Brylcreem to stick it flat, and the suit I got is old-fashioned. It's navy-blue double-breasted and the trousers are a bit too short now I've got taller. A lot of the lads have got gaberdine suits with a full drape and single button. And they wears silk ties with patterns and pictures on them just like the Yanks wear in the films, and suede brothel-creeper shoes with thick sponge soles. They looks ever so good.

Johnny Merry says that I ought to shave all me hair off, and then it would grow nicer than it is now. But me Mam won't let me. She reckons that I'll look like I come out of Belsen if I shave me hair off, because she says there's more meat on a sparrow's kneecaps than there is on me.

Johnny Merry is my best pal, you know. We've been best pals ever since we was little kids. Except for the time he was in the Approved School. Oh yeah, he got sent away for a long time. He lives with his big sister, Doreen, you see, and the police said that she couldn't control him, so they sent him to an Approved School down in a place called Chepstow. But he's been back home for ages.

He's got a green gaberdine suit with a full drape and a single button, and blue suede brothel-creepers and a tie with a picture of a filmstar on it. His hair is all long and wavy. He's really good-looking and a lot of the girls likes him. But he don't care about any of them. He says that they're all local yokels and he's Big-Time, a City Slicker. He says that he's going to be a gangster in America like George Raft and James Cagney.

Just for now though he's working in a factory. But he don't like it. He says it's ever so boring. He's on a machine that stamps out tin lids for jam jars, one at a time. He reckons he's stamped out five million lids since he's been working there. He says there's an old bloke working on the machine next to him who's been stamping out lids for fifty years. He calls the old bloke the 'Zombie', because he reckons he's dead really, but he won't lie down. Johnny says the Zombie is there stamping when he comes to work in the morning and he never speaks or looks at anybody all day, and he never stops work and when Johnny goes home at night the Zombie is still there stamping. Johnny says that his Foreman told him the Zombie had died in 1934, but when they buried him he come back out of the grave that same night and next morning they found him at the stamping machine working away like mad. So the Boss just kept quiet about it and let the Zombie go on working. The Boss says he's the ideal Working Man. Slaves away day and night, never gets stroppy, and never asks for a pay rise.

Anyway, I was telling you about the gaberdine suits, wasn't I? Well, I asked me Mam if she could lend me the money so I could get a gaberdine suit, but she told me to sod off. Then, a bit later on, she said, 'I'll tell you what I'll do, Specs. You give me some money every week to save for you, and I'll help you to get a gaberdine suit. I'll give you some money towards it when you've saved half what it'll cost.'

So I stopped going to the dances at the Memorial Hall, and I stayed in nearly every night for weeks, and I give me Mam ten shillings on top of me keep every Friday for weeks and weeks. You see, I get two pounds fifteen shillings a week wages, and I have to give me Mam two pounds for me keep, and with the other fifteen I have to buy anything I want. So giving her ten shillings extra meant I only had five bob a week left.

Then one Saturday afternoon I was with Fatty Polson looking in the shops down town and I saw this smashing gaberdine suit. All brown and shiny, with full drape and single button, and it said 'Special Offer' on it, so I went inside and asked the man how much it was.

'Nine pounds, six shillings,' he told me, and that if I put down five pounds deposit I could pay the rest off at five bob a week. He said he'd sell me a silk tie with a picture as well at so much a week, and a shirt with long collar points, just like the Yanks wear in the pictures. And then he said he just happened to have some brothel-creepers in stock as well. They were the very latest fashion, all purple-coloured with red tassels on the laces' ends. He said I could pay for them weekly as well, but I'd got to put five pounds down as deposit before I could have any of the things.

I wasn't half excited, because I knew that I'd give me Mam six pounds ten shillings altogether to save for me. I only had four shillings with me, so he took that for keeping the suit for me until I could bring back the deposit money.

I run all the way home and me Mam and Sid were sitting in the kitchen drinking beer.

'I want me money, Mam,' I said. 'I've found a smashing suit. I shan't need to have any money from you neither, because the man told me that I can pay the rest off at five bob a week.'

She looked all shocked, and blinked at me like she does when she can't think of nothing to say. Mind you, that don't happen very often.

I could already see meself in the gaberdine suit and the purple brothel-creepers going to the Memorial Hall that night and asking Glenda Shortway to dance with me. I bet she'll think I look really good in me new clothes. Really fashionable and Big Time City Slicker. I'll ask her to be my girlfriend after the dance, and then I'll walk her home, and we'll have a snog in her doorway.

We'll get married and go shopping together every Saturday afternoon, and to the Memorial Hall dance every Saturday night, and to the pictures every Sunday. Of course, if me and Glenda Shortway are getting married I shan't be able to join the Foreign Legion, will I. But that don't matter. I'd sooner marry Glenda Shortway than go marching over the desert sands to get killed in Fort Zinderneuf.

'Come on, Mam, give me me money. The shop 'ull be closed else before I can get back there.'

She went all red and slitted her eyes like she does when she gets mad.

'Don't you come giving me orders, you cheeky young bleeder.'

'I'm not.' She still scares me a bit when she goes mad, you know. 'Only the man's keeping the suit for me, and he says I've got to collect it today or else he'll sell it to somebody else.'

'I'm not standing for some bloody tupenny ha'penny shopkeeper threatening me!' she skreeked. 'You can tell him to shove his bloody suit where the monkey keeps his nuts.'

I can't take this in, you know. Why she's playing up like this, I mean. But before I can say anything she jumps up and skreeks, 'I'm going out. I can't stand any more of this. I'm going to find a bit of peace and quiet.'

And she goes roaring out of the house and down the street.

Sid glares at me. 'Look what you've done now, Specs. Why do you want to go and upset your Mam like that for?'

I can't take this in. I go out of the house, and I'm feeling really down in the mouth. I could cry when I think of how I was going to go to the dance tonight and make Glenda Shortway my girlfriend. There's no chance now of that, is there. Glenda won't even look at me if I'm wearing my rotten old navy-blue double-breasted, will she.

Johnny Merry comes along then and sees me mooching about.

'What's up, Specs? You looks like you've lost a pound and found a penny.'

So I tell him what's happened.

'I can't take it in, Johnny. Why me Mam went mad like that. I only wanted me own money back from her.'

'She can't give you your money because she's spent it, Specs. That's what's happened, I'll bet me life on it.'

'What?' I can't believe what he's said.

'I'm telling you, that's what she's done. Go and ask her if you don't believe me.'

'But how does you know?' I ask him, and he winks all sly.

'I learned a lot at that Approved School I went to, Specs.'

Do you know, Johnny Merry knows things that I've never ever thought of ... He really is a Big Time City Slicker, aren't he ...

Anyway, when I got back home me Mam is there talking to Hilda, me Uncle Harold's girlfriend, and when I come in Hilda looks all sorrowful at me and shakes her head.

'How could you do this, Specs, after all that your poor Mam has done for you? Look at all the sacrifices she's made to bring you up and give you the best of everything, and now you turn on her like this. How could you, Specs?'

I don't know what she's on about. I haven't done anything to me Mam, have I.

Then me Mam starts to cry and wail

and keeps skreeking, 'I wish I was dead. I wish I was laying in me grave. I never thought I'd live to see the day that me own son treated me so cruel. Trying to rob me of me last few pennies after all I'se give to him.'

'There, there, now, Effie. Don't you take on so. There, there, there, now.' Hilda is bending over her, stroking her head and patting her shoulders, and glaring daggers at me.

I can't take it in, I really can't. What have I done? All I did was to ask for me own money back!

Three

I'm fed up with living at home, I really am. I'm still sleeping on the front room couch, because me Dad is still using me camp-bed. Me Mam has moved Virgy into the attic to share with Hilda, and Sid is sleeping in the back bedroom with Uncle Harold. Because me Mam says that she can't make up her mind whether to try being married to me Dad again, or whether to stay with Sid. In the meantime she's going to sleep by herself.

Me Dad's been home for weeks now and his money still hasn't come from Australia. Neither has his luggage.

Sid keeps making nasty remarks about it, and every morning he gets up early and waits for the postman to see if he's bringing any parcels or letters for me Dad. Nothing ever comes and then Sid asks me Dad, 'Is it the Boomerang post that your money's coming by, Horace?'

Me Dad looks all fierce and says, 'What d'you mean by that, Sidney?'

Sid smiles all silkily. 'That sort of post that turns round and goes back before it arrives, Horace.'

And Sid keeps on asking him, 'Tell me, Horace, that ship that's bringing your luggage? It's not by any chance called the *Titanic*, is it?'

When he says that me Dad curls his upper lip like Humphrey Bogart and tells him, 'Just watch it, Tompkin, you punk! You're messing with dynamite when you mess with me.'

But now Sid's seen how weedy me Dad is he's not scared of him anymore. At least, he acts as if he's not scared, because he always does his James Cagney imitation.

'Lissen, Horace Kensal, in the war I ate dirty rats like you for breakfast every day, and three times a day on a Sunday.'

But they always stands right away from each other and just keeps on growling things like:

'Just you try it, Punk. I'll make mincemeat of you.'

'Oh yeah? Just you try it, you Dirty Rat! I'll make raw liver of you.'

'Oh yeah? Just you try it, Wise Guy. I'll make a dog's dinner of you.'

'Oh yeah? Just you try it, Meat Yed. I'll ate you raw.'

They goes on for hours like that until me Mam comes in and skreeks at them. 'Just shurrup, the pair of you, I'm sick of you fighting over me.'

But I reckon that she only pretends to be mad at them. I reckon she likes it really when they have a go at each other over her, because when they're not there she tells Hilda ever so smugly, 'Those two were fighting over me again, Hilda. I've always driven men mad with desire for me, you know.'

And Hilda always looks a bit jealous when she says that, and tells her, 'No,

Effie, I didn't know.'

Me Mam gets all spiteful then. 'Of course, our Harold 'ud never fight over you, would he, Hilda. So you haven't got any idea what it's like to have such power over men as I've got. To be able to drive them mad with desire to possess you.'

Hilda gets all snotty then. 'My Harold is a gentleman. Not a scruffy hooligan like them two are. Fighting is beneath him, he says.'

Me Mam snorts all contemptuous then. 'Humph! Our Harold's always been soft. And soft-yedded as well. That's why you got hold of him in the first place. He knows that any glamorous woman like me wouldn't even look at him. We likes real men.'

And Hilda always goes all red in the face, and looks like she's going to cry. And when me Mam sees that she always gets all sorry for Hilda, and tries to be ever so nice to her, and they're friends again then.

I feel sorry for Hilda as well. She looks all old and withered, and she always wears a turban and trousers and Uncle Harold's old overcoat. And she always smells of factory-oil, and wears her hair in curlers.

Mind you, I don't know where me Mam

gets off acting as if she's a film star, and talking about being a glamorous woman. She's all haggard and skinny and only got a few teeth. And she has to put thick paint on her face to hide her pimples. And her hair is dyed yellow. I know it's dyed because the roots are always a different colour from the rest of it. And she has it in curlers nearly all the time as well.

I haven't told you about me Uncle Harold and Hilda yet, have I.

Uncle Harold is me Mam's brother, and Hilda is his fiancée. They've been going to get married for years and years, but every time they name a date, just before it comes round Uncle Harold has one of his nervous breakdowns.

Only they haven't named a date for a long time now, because Uncle Harold says they can't afford to get married because Smiling Sam the Coffin Man won't give him a pay rise. Me Mam says that that's a load of bollocks, and that Uncle Harold is just making excuses to avoid taking on the responsibilities of Holy Matrimony.

Smiling Sam is the Undertaker and he always says he's the happiest, jolliest undertaker in the whole of Christendom.

He's always singing and laughing, especially when there's a lot of people dying, because he says that when business is thriving it's the time for rejoicing. Uncle Harold started working for him when the war was on.

In the war, you see, me Uncle Harold was told he was going to have to be a Bevin Boy and work in the coalmines. He couldn't go into the Forces because of his nervous breakdowns. That's why he left the Home Guards because the sergeant shouted at him one day and give him a nervous breakdown. He hadn't never worked neither, because every time someone found him a job he had a nervous breakdown. But he used to love to go and sit in the cemetery, he said the company there was so polite and genteel and quiet, so me Mam got him a job with Smiling Sam, and Uncle Harold loved it. All he had to do was dress up in a black tailcoat and top hat and walk in front of the funeral procession, and afterwards stand and weep at the graveside, if there wasn't anybody else there to cry over the coffin. He did ever so well, and Smiling Sam promoted him to be the Director of Burial Music and Ceremony.

Uncle Harold recruited a band. He had Tommy TeeTee with his tambourine and Bertie Shellshock with his tin drum, and they used to play at all the funerals.

Bertie Shellshock was blown up by a shell in the first war and it turned him Doolally Tap. He likes to walk around the town all day banging on his tin drum, and some people gives him money because they're sorry for him. Some gives him money to go away because the noise he makes gets on their nerves.

My Mam always says that she reckons she's getting shellshock when Bertie Shellshock starts hammering that bleedin' drum.

Uncle Harold never played any instrument. He used to wear a long black cloak and wave a broomstick like a Drum Major, and he'd hum the tunes. He can imitate a trumpet as well, and he'd do the Last Post by special request. But he always had to have a few days off sick after doing the Last Post, because the strain of it made him feel all weak and weary. He had to stop having the band at the funerals though, because Tommy TeeTee is always drunk and he kept on falling down into the grave on top of the coffins, and sometimes the relatives of the dead 'uns got all mad about that.

Uncle Harold was very upset at losing Tommy TeeTee, because Tommy always wore his Salvation Army uniform and polished his wellies for the funerals, and Uncle Harold said it added a touch of Martial splendour to the ceremony.

Tommy TeeTee isn't really in the Salvation Army, but he goes to the Army Hall every Sunday night and swears he's been redeemed and he's turned Teetotal and he'll never drink again. And they gives him their old uniforms to wear. He's ever so small though, so he has to roll up the sleeves and trousers, and the jacket always hangs down to his knees. They give him his tambourine as well, and he can't half play it. He can do all the flourishes and twirls with the ribbons better than any of the Songster Brigade.

After Uncle Harold and Tommy TeeTee and Bertie Shellshock was stopped from playing at funerals they tried to get some gigs around the town. But the only place that they can get gigs at is the Old People's Sunshine Care Home down Arnus Street.

A woman who works there told me, 'All the poor old buggers have got Alzheimers

Disease, and they thinks it's Henry Mancini and His Orchestra playing to them ...'

Granny Smith, me Mam's mam, had that disease, Alzheimers. She's dead now. Me Mam was upset when Granny Smith died but nobody else was because she was horrible.

Uncle Harold said, 'Of course it is regrettable that Mother should have passed away, but I have to confess that the release from the purgatory of scratching her back fills me with joy.'

He always talks a bit funny like that, you know.

But not having to scratch Granny Smith's back anymore fills me with joy as well. She used to make me stand for hours and hours with me hand down inside her dress scratching her back, it was all sweaty and horrible and pimply, and when I used to get tired and want to stop she wouldn't let me. She used to threaten to tell me Mam about the time that she'd caught me playing with meself in the lavatory. That used to scare me, because me Mam always said that if boys played with themselves they'd go blind, or mad, or both, and that if she ever found out that I was playing with meself she'd chop my willie off.

When I was small I believed what she said about what would happen to me if I played with meself. But Johnny Merry told me that it was all a load of old codswallop. He said that in the Approved School the lads used to make a circle and have wanking competitions to see who could come the quickest. Johnny Merry told me that boys who didn't play with themselves turned into Poofs and them Dirty Old Men who interferes with little kids in the pictures when it's all dark. So now I don't take any notice of what my Mam told me because I don't want to turn into a Poof or a Dirty Old Man.

It was weird the night that Granny Smith died in the back bedroom. She said that she wanted her family around her, so we all had to go up and stand around the bed. Except for our Virgy, because she'd gone to the pictures with her mates. Uncle Sid never come up neither, because he was too scared to come up with the rest of us in case he caught something from Granny Smith, so he went to the pub instead. And Hilda never come, because Granny Smith said that she didn't want Hilda to be there because she was the Scarlet Whore of Babylon who had ensnared her innocent son, Harold, into the paths of wickedness and debauchery.

So in the end there was only me and Uncle Harold and my Mam there.

When we was round her bed Granny Smith told us, 'My Albert's waiting for me, you know. He's come to take me to Heaven.'

Albert was her husband, and he's been dead for years and years.

'Don't talk so sarft, Mam,' me Mam told her all sharpish.

Me Mam gets scared of spooky things, you see, and she don't like to hear anybody talking about them.

Uncle Harold was ever so interested though. 'Has Father really come to see you, Mother? Could you perhaps be more specific? I'd like to hear the details of his journey here, and his present existence such as his diet, leisure activities, et cetera.'

Uncle Harold wanted to know all the details because he's writing a book about his experiences in the Undertaking business and 'any fully authenticated meeting with a Departed One would add colour and excitement'. That's what he says! He always talks like that, you know.

'Well, ask him yourself, you gormless

bugger,' Granny Smith told him all snotty.

'How can I do that, Mother?' Uncle Harold's glasses were beginning to steam up because he was getting really excited.

'Just open your mouth,' Granny Smith said, 'And ask him yourself. There he is, standing outside the window there. Only don't let the bugger come inside because he brings a cold wind with him.'

'Ohhhh Gooodddddd!' me Mam skreeked. 'She's gone off her yed properly this time. I'm going to fetch the doctor to her and have her committed.'

Me and Uncle Harold run across to the window and looked out, but there was nothing there, and anyway we was too high up from the ground for anybody to be able to stand outside the window, wasn't we.

Uncle Harold was ever so disappointed, so was I as well. I'd have liked to have seen Grandad Smith, it would have been an adventure to tell Johnny Merry about. It's not fair really, because Johnny Merry is always having adventures that he can tell me about, and I never have any adventures that I can tell him about.

'There's nobody here, Mother,' Uncle Harold told her.

'O' course there is, you silly blind bleeder.' Granny Smith got all riled up then. 'My Albert is staring you right in your bloody gormless face.'

She sounded so certain that I had to look again to see if Grandad Smith really wasn't there. The window was a bit dirty and hard to see out of, so I opened it, and a big gust of cold wind blew in, and Granny Smith bawled art me.

'You stupid young bugger, I told you not to let him in, didn't I. Now he's brought the cold in with him.' Then she shook her fist at the wall by the side of the bed and shouted, 'No, you aren't getting into my bed, Albert Smith. I've been a virgin for twenty-odd years, and that's how I'm going to stay. So you can keep your mucky hands to yourself, and your other mucky bits as well.'

My Mam skreeked real loud. 'Ooohhhh my Goooddddd! She's gone stark raving bonkers. Fetch the doctor somebody. I'm going to get her put away for good this time.'

Uncle Harold took his glasses off and wiped them, and then put them back on and went peering real close at the wall.

'Get off my Albert's foot, you gormless

sod,' Granny Smith shouted at him. 'Can't you hear him shouting? Youm stood right on his bad toe.'

Uncle Harold's face was all glowing with excitement. 'I do apologise, Father ... Isn't this wonderful, Specs! We are in the presence of a 'Departed One'. What a sublime chapter it will make for my book.'

'Ask Grandad Smith if he can show himself a bit clearer to us?' I told Uncle Harold, and me Mam skreeked, 'You've all gone bloody mad. I'm going to fetch the doctor to the lot of you.'

And she run downstairs and out along the street and I could hear her bawling, 'They're all mad! They're all bloody stark raving bonkers!'

Granny Smith grinned all sly at the wall then. 'Did you hear what that silly cow was skreeking, Albert, my love? She reckons she's fetching the doctor to get me put away for good. Well, she's left it a bit too late, aren't she, Albert. We'll be well gone before she gets back here. So Tarra all.'

She lay back with a big sly grin all over her face, closed her eyes, and died, just like that. And all the curtains blew right out of the window just as if somebody was dragging them outside with them.

I felt a bit scared then, but Uncle Harold was chuckling and rubbing his hands and telling me, 'Superb, Specs! Absolutely superb! When people read this chapter in my book it will create a sensation. Superb, Specs, absolutely superb ... And just think, my boy. No more back-scratching to do! Not one solitary pimple to be scratched anymore. Superb, Specs! Superb!'

Thinking about that, I couldn't help but feel a bit cheery meself ...

And then Granny Smith spoiled it all. She opened her eyes, sat up in bed and laughing like a witch told us, 'Had you gormless buggers all fooled that time, didn't I. You won't get rid o'me that easy. I've told Albert to come and fetch me next week instead. Now get scratching, Specs.'

I could have really cried then ...

She kept me there scratching her back for hours and hours.

Then the next night I went to the pictures, and when I come back all the neighbours was in the house, and me Mam and Virgy and Hilda was all skreeking and Uncle Harold told me that me Granny

Smith had died while I was out.

Funny enough, I felt all sad and cried a bit meself then.

You ought to see Uncle Harold in his funeral clothes though. He's tall and skinny, and he wears glasses and his hair is all black and bushy, but when he's dressed up in his top hat and tailcoat and long black cloak he looks really distinguished, just like one of those diplomats. Smiling Sam loves him, he says he's really good at his job and always suggesting new ideas for the funerals.

Smiling Sam reckons Uncle Harold's latest idea is a real cracker. It's a portable cemetery. So that you can have the burial at home, or in the pub, or wherever you want it. Uncle Harold has already designed it and applied for the patent, and Smiling Sam is going to go into partnership with him to produce it. Uncle Harold's keeping it all a big secret though, until he's got the patent granted and he's ready to go into full production. He says he doesn't want to risk some smart shyster pinching his idea, so he won't tell anybody yet what his design is like.

Another idea he had was for Hilda to

dress up in long black veils, cover herself all over with them, and stand waiting in the cemetery gateway for the funeral procession to come. She was supposed to represent the 'Spirit of Death' welcoming the new arrival.

Hilda didn't really want to do it because she's very shy, and me Mam scotched that one. She told Harold he was a creepy morbid bastard, and if he made Hilda do it, me Mam 'ud have his guts for garters. So he had to abandon that idea.

He was very disappointed though. He told me, 'Do you know, Specs, there are times I despair of your mother. She has no artistry in her soul. She just cannot appreciate the poetic beauty of my visionary inspiration.'

He was so upset that he started to cry, and his glasses steamed up so thick I had to lead him home again because he couldn't see where he was going.

I like Uncle Harold. He's ever so sensitive, and he wouldn't harm a fly. But me Mam always says when she looks at him, that it's easy to see why the flies thinks he's a landing strip ...

Four

It's ever so boring round here. There's nothing to do at nights. It's alright for the old blokes, because they can go to the pub, but when I go into the pub the landlord always tells me to get out because I'm too young.

I go to the Memorial Hall dance on Saturday nights, and to the pictures on Sunday nights, and most of the other nights I go to the Youth Club, but it's boring because it's always the same every week, and I want to be travelling the world having adventures.

The bloke who runs the Youth Club is called Donald Dunmow and he's a Scotchman. He don't like any of our gang, especially me and Johnny Merry, because we sings that song:

'Oh I just come in from the Isle of Skye
And I'm noo very big and I'm awful shy.
All the lasses shout Hey Hi,
Donald, where's your trooosers?'

And we keep on asking him to let us have a Boxing Club there. But all he wants us to do is to play table-tennis and have discussions about politics and religion, and train spotting, and learn soft girly things like flower arranging and model-making, and to go on Nature Rambles in the woods and fields.

Donald Dunmow says that he doesn't want roughs and scruffs like us in his Youth Club, and that he'd bar us from going there if he could. He tried to bar us once and we hadn't done nothing wrong at all, and Johnny Merry's big sister Doreen went to see one of the Councillors that she knows. He's a old bloke named Albert Harper, and my Mam reckons that he's Doreen's Fancy Man. Her and Doreen had a row one day and my Mam told Doreen she should be ashamed of herself for having old Albert Harper for her Sugar Daddy, and him married with eight grown-up kids.

Doreen told her, 'You'm just jealous, Effie Kensal, because nobody wants to be your Sugar Daddy. It's the same as in the war, aren't it, when you couldn't get a Yank, you was jealous of me then as well because I could have any Yank I wanted for me boyfriend.'

'Me, jealous?' Me Mam went all haughty then. 'Me jealous of you? Let me tell you, Lady, I had too much self-respect to go chasing after the bloody Yanks like you did.'

'I'se never had to chase after men. Men has aways chased after me.' Doreen was rocking her head and looking all pleased with herself.

'Only because youm so easy to catch. The men knows that they only has to chase you a tiny bit of the way and they're onto a sure thing.'

Me Mam went back into the house then very quick, because she knew she'd got a good one in there, and didn't want to give Doreen the chance to get one back.

Anyway, like I was saying, Doreen went to see Albert Harper, and he's the Councillor who's in charge of the Recreation Committee, and the Recreation Committee is the boss of Donald Dunmow. Albert Harper went to see Dunmow and told him that he'd got to let our gang use the Youth Club so long as we was behaving ourselves in a orderly fashion. So Dunmow has to let us stay as club members, but he hates it. His eyes glows all red when he sees us walk in, and if ever any of us speaks to him, he just looks straight through us, and his hands clench into fists. So me and Johnny Merry always keeps on going up to him and asking him things like:

'When is the next Nature Ramble, Mr Dunmow? We should like to come with you on that. And could you show us how to arrange the flowers this week, we find it ever so very interesting. And guess what we spotted last week at the Junction? We spotted Engine number 123456.'

He just stands there looking through us and biting his lips, and clenching his fists.

Glenda Shortway comes to the club sometimes. But she's always with her mates and she don't talk to any of our gang. She looks at me sometimes, but when I look back she looks away and then her mates all looks at me and laughs. It makes me feel all daft, that does, and I can feel me face going red when they does it.

I don't tell anybody that I like Glenda Shortway and want to marry her, because they'll only take the mickey out of me for being so soft and soppy.

Johnny Merry reckons he's never going to get married. He says that when he goes to be a gangster in America he'll have film stars for his girlfriends, like George Raft and James Cagney and Humphrey Bogart do in the films.

We only like Yankee films, you know. The British films are terrible, but the Yankee films are ever so good.

I went to see Errol Flynn last week, in *They Died with Their Boots On*. It was all about Custer's Last Stand.

Sid and me Dad had a row about it, because me Mam said that she wanted to go and see it. She likes Errol Flynn, you see.

Sid said, 'What does you want to go and see that bloody fairy for, when you'se got a real man at home?'

'Yeah, that's right,' me Dad said. 'And his name is Horace Kensal.'

'Horace Kensal?' Sid was all sneery. 'Who the bloody hell has kidded Horace Kensal that he's a real man?'

'The same people who knew Horace Kensal when he was fighting for his country, and carving out an empire for himself in the Australian Outback.' Me Dad looked ever so smug when he said that.

'Outback?' Sid shot back. 'The only

bloody Outback Horace Kensal has ever been in is that bloody backyard out there that you can see through the window. And the nearest he ever got to the war was watching the bloody planes take off and land.'

'Would you kindly ask Sidney Tompkin to show me his medals from the war,' me Dad asked me Mam. 'Only I've heard a rumour that he never got any, because all he did in the war was to sit on his arse here at home.'

'Effie, my dearest, would you tell Horace Kensal that Sidney Tompkin's medals are being held at Buckingham Palace until he gets permission from Winston Churchill to tell about the deeds of daring he done during the war.'

'Oh, shurrup the pair of you!' me Mam raved like a maniac. 'I'm sick and tired of both of you. I'm going to see Errol Flynn by meself.'

She went storming out, and then Uncle Harold piped up.

'Might I make a suggestion?'

'Feel free, Harold,' me Dad said all sarcastic. 'I'm sure that any suggestion you make will be well worth listening to.'

'Well, it has occurred to me that the

solution to your problem is to fight a duel. That is what Gentlemen normally do in your situation.'

'I'd fight a duel this minute if I could find a gentleman to fight it with.' Me Dad put on his posh voice. When he does that me Mam always tells him he sounds like a prat, but he thinks he sounds ever so good and High and Mighty. 'But there's only one gentleman here, and that's me.'

'Oh, is that so?' Sid got all narked then. 'Well, let me tell you, Kensal, that I comes from a very old and noble family. The Tompkins has always been counted as Aristocracy. And the Tompkins has had more duels than any other family in the land.'

Me Dad laughed all nasty. 'The only duel a Tompkin has ever fought was when your Mam was fighting the coppers who come to arrest her for being drunk and disorderly.'

'That's it! You'se gone too far this time, Kensal.' Sid banged his fists on the table and jumped up. He was trying to hold his breath and push his chest out, but he's so weedy there's more meat on a bike chain. 'Name your weapons, Kensal.'

Me Dad jumped up then and tried to

look tough. But he's as weedy as Sid, and he looked just like a rabid mouse.

'Anything you wants, Tompkin,' he hissed like a snake does, only it sounded funny because he hadn't got his teeth in. 'Guns, swords, knives, battleaxes, anything you wants.'

'Wait a minute, wait a minute,' Uncle Harold told them. 'Just calm down now, will you. There's a proper procedure to be followed here, you know. You can't just carry on like this. You have to follow the proper procedure.

'The challenge has to be formally issued by the aggrieved party's seconds, and then the one who's been challenged has the choice of weapons and also a choice of venue. Now since Sid is the challenger, it's all up to Horace to choose the venue and weapons.'

'That aren't fair for a start,' Sid said. 'Why should he have a venue and not me?'

'Because I was badly wounded in the war, that's why I needs a venue,' me Dad said.

Well, it seems only fair to me. If he was wounded in the war he deserves to have something extra to use in the duel, don't he.

'Oh no! I aren't having that.' Sid was shaking his head and puffing his cheeks out. 'I'm not going to let him have a venue and not me. It aren't right, that aren't. Besides, how does we know that he was badly wounded in the war? Where's the scars?'

'That's for me to know, and for you not to know.' Me Dad was all smug. 'My war wounds am private.'

'Probably because they'm all on your arse.' Sid smirked all triumphant. 'I expect you got 'um when you was running away from the enemy.'

'You've gone too far now, Tompkins.' Me Dad was roaring mad now. 'I'm going to make raw liver out of you.'

'Phoooo! You and whose army? Just you try it!' Sid was prancing up and down and waving his fists in the air like a boxer. 'I warn't a middle-weight champion for nothing, you know. I'll make mincemeat out of you.'

'Come on then. You're talking to the Champion of Australia. I'se beat the best, I has.' Me Dad was jumping around on his side of the table, waving his fists in front of him like a boxer.

Then they both started throwing punches,

but because the table was between them their arms wasn't long enough and all the punches just hit the air over the table.

Then they both got tired out and flopped down onto their chairs gasping and panting.

Uncle Harold was all white and trembly. 'I reckon one of my nervous breakdowns is coming on, Specs,' he told me all pitiful. 'I'm too sensitive to witness such terrible violence.'

Well, to be honest I reckon that two gnats could have done more damage to each other than these two have. They never got nearer to each other than at least a yard apart.

But I felt sorry for Uncle Harold so I took him down to the cemetery so he could enjoy himself reading all the tombstones, and I let him tell me all about his favourite funerals.

After he was feeling better he said, 'I'm considering letting you into my most closely guarded secret, Specs, because I know that I can rely upon your absolute discretion. Absolutely.'

He likes that word 'Absolutely', you know. He uses it a lot. If you say to him, 'The weather's nice today', he says,

'Yes it is, Specs, absolutely.' And if you tell him, 'The Prime Minister is going to put up the taxes again,' he says, 'It is absolutely necessary, Specs.' And if you ask him, 'Do you want a cup of tea, Uncle Harold?' he nods and says, 'Absolutely, Specs. Absolutely.'

The word he liked best before he liked 'absolutely' was 'indupisidately', but I don't know what that means, and I can't find it in the dictionary, so I think it must be one of Uncle Harold's inventions.

Anyway, it's his new invention which is his most closely guarded secret. The portable cemetery. And he tells me, 'As a reward for your constant loyalty and friendship towards myself, Specs, I am going to show you the prototype of my new invention.'

In the middle of the cemetery there's an old chapel which isn't used anymore, and all the seats and everything have been took out so there's lots of room inside it. Uncle Harold has got the key to it and he takes me up there now and we go inside.

'There, Specs. There it is. I call it "The Sweet Dreams Mobile Resting Haven."'

Uncle Harold's eyes are tearful he's so proud of his new invention.

It's a long, deep, wooden box sitting on eight pairs of pram wheels, and he's nailed a load of old paper-flowered wreaths all over it. It's got long poles sticking out from the front and back.

'That's the shafts for the horses, or for the bearers to push and pull it along, Specs. And you see these two small chariots, don't you ...' he shows me two old prams with paper flowers stuck all over them, '... These are to transport the earth in.'

He's grinning ever so proud.

'What we shall do, when I receive the patent, is to offer the "At Home Burial Service". It will be advertised as being particularly suitable in times of inclement weather. Why go out in the cold and rain to stand in a windswept, freezing cemetery getting wet through and catching cold, when there is this alternative? A burial performed in the warmth and comfort of One's own home ... Just look at this, Specs.'

He's full of enthusiasm. And he rushes to unbolt the side of the box and lift it down.

'There, you see that, Specs? What could be more convenient? No need to lower a heavy coffin into a deep grave, with all the concomitant dangers of dislocating one's back. Instead one merely removes the side of the box, slides the coffin into it, then replaces the side and gets on with the service. The earth will be carried in the chariots in convenient small bags which can be easily lifted and put down onto the coffin, again without any undue muscular strain or exertion.

'I've also foreseen the need for tasteful memorial tombstones which can be placed on top of the burial mound immediately. These will be made of papier mâché. I visualise a catalogue displaying a wide and tasteful range of headstones, angels, cherubs, Grecian urns, et cetera. Now, Specs, what do you think of it? Is it not absolutely brilliant?'

'Absolutely, Uncle Harold.' But there's one thing that's puzzling me a bit, so I ask him, 'But where will you park it when it's full?'

'Ahahhh!' He looks really smug, and he taps the side of his nose with his finger. 'Ah haa, Specs. See this lever here at the front, and this hinged hatch on the rear. Now watch this.'

He pulled the lever and the front end

lifted up high and the hinged flap on the rear swung open.

'This is the Piece de Resistance of my conception, though I say so myself, Specs. The grave-diggers will have a grave ready dug for us, so upon our arrival at the static cemetery we just line the mobile up with the end of the hole, I pull the lever in front, and Hey Presto! The Dear Departed slides neatly out of the rear and down into the hole. Nothing could be simpler, easier, or more speedy. And all done with the very utmost degree of good taste and decorum.'

You have to admit it, Uncle Harold is really clever in his own way, arn't he!

'And the beauty of it is, Specs, is that the grave-diggers will use the dirt they've took out of the grave to fill it in. So all the bags of dirt can be put back into the chariots and used again and again. So can the papier mâché tombstones and ornaments. What economy, Specs! Smiling Sam says that his profit margin on our "At Home" burials will be immense, and he's promised me a substantial commission on each one that we do, plus a percentage of the profits.'

He started staring at me then, as if he was thinking of something. And then he told me, 'There's a great future in Death for any young man of enterprise and initiative, Specs. Would you like me to have a word with Smiling Sam about finding you employment as part of our Portable Cemetery team?'

Well, I like Uncle Harold ever so much, and I don't like hurting his feelings at all, but I don't fancy running about all day with a Portable Cemetery tipping coffins into graves. So I tell him, 'Well, thank you very much for the offer, Uncle Harold. But me Mam wants me to stay on the Gas. She says I've got a job for life there.'

'Phoooey!' Uncle Harold waved his hand in the air all dismissive and contemptuous. 'I'm not offering you a job, Specs. I'm offering you a career. The sky's the limit!

'Has your Mam not considered the fact that there might well be other energy sources which will replace gas in the future? Where will you be then, when that day comes? I'll tell you where you'll be, Specs. You'll be on the scrapheap of unemployment. But as part of the Portable Cemetery Team, you are assured of a lifelong career. After all, Specs, people are never going to stop dying, are they? It's not like an energy source, is it. There's no alternative to it, as far as can be ascertained.'

Well, I know that for a fact already, don't I. But I don't want to spend every day being reminded of it, do I. So I tell him, 'Can I have some time to think it over, Uncle Harold?'

He smiled all graciously. 'But of course you can, my dear Specs. But try not to take too long about coming to your decision, will you? Who knows when you yourself may be summoned to your own Last Resting Place. It would be a tragedy if you were summoned before you took advantage of the offer I'm making.'

I just nodded, but to tell you the truth I shan't be going down to the cemetery with Uncle Harold again in a hurry. It's beginning to give me the Willies!

Five

I was sent with Georgie Snood to do a job at Solly Pig's house today. That's not his real name, Solly Pig, it's Solly Thompson really, but everybody calls him Solly Pig because he keeps a lot of pigs in some big sties at the back of his house. He looks like a pig as well, all fat and greasy and muddy, and he stinks of pig muck, and he don't speak to you, he grunts. Everybody says he's pig-ignorant. But he's got a lot of money so everybody is crawly to him to his face.

Georgie Snood is a real crawler, you know. When he talks to the Boss at the Gas, Mr Thrall, he calls him Sir, and it's all 'Yes, Sir. No, Sir. Three bags full, Sir.' Then behind the Boss's back he cusses and swears about him, and says, 'If that bugger Thrall spoke to me like he speaks to some of the other chaps I'd knock him into the middle of next week.'

Well, one morning in front of all of us Mr Thrall told Georgie Snood, 'You stupid bugger, Snood, you're bloody useless. Next time you mess any job up I'll kick your arse all down the street. Does you hear me, you stupid, useless bugger?'

And Georgie Snood said, 'Yes, Sir. No, Sir. Three bags full, Sir.'

Afterwards I asked Georgie, 'Why didn't you knock Mr Thrall into the middle of next week, then?'

He went bloody mad, and come after

me with a hammer. I didn't half run fast, I'll tell you.

Anyway, me and Georgie Snood went to Solly Thompson's house, but nobody answered the front door so we went round the back where all the pigsties are. Nobody come to the back door neither, so Georgie told me, 'Go down the sties and see if Solly Pig's there.'

All the pigs come looking to see who it was. They was grunting and snuffling and jumping up with their front trotters on the walls to look at me, and Georgie Snood shouted, 'Watch they don't drag you into the sty and ate you, Specs. The last mate I brought here ended up as a pig's dinner. All we ever found of him was his teeth.'

I knew he was only trying to scare me, but some of the pigs was really big, and the way they was looking at me and grunting I was beginning to get a bit nervous the further I went into the sties. So I stood still and shouted for Solly Thompson.

I could hear one pig squealing ever so loud and then it stopped and Solly Thompson come roaring out of a sty, all red and sweaty.

'Who the bleeding hell are you? What's you doing here? Has my bloody Missus sent you to spy on me? I'll feed you to my pigs, you skinny little bleeder! I'll teach you to spy on me!'

'I'm not a spy. I'm on the Gas,' I told him, but he kept on roaring and coming so I run back to where Georgie Snood was.

When Solly Thompson come up to us Georgie Snood took his cap off and said, 'Good morning, Sir. Come to fix your gas leak, I have.'

Solly was glaring all suspicious at me. 'Who's that?'

'He's supposed to be helping me,' Georgie Snood said all sneery. 'Though for all the use he is, I'd do better to have one of your pigs mating me.'

That was a rotten thing to say, wasn't it. He'd sooner have a pig helping him than me. Well, he needn't worry, because that's exactly what I feel. I'd sooner be mating a pig than him.

'How long have you been here?' Solly Thompson was glaring all suspicious at both of us now.

'Just this minute, Sir,' Georgie told him.

'Are you sure?'

'Yes, Sir, come just this minute we have. I do hope it's convenient, Sir. If it's not convenient then I'll be happy to come back again at whatever time suits you, Sir.'

Aren't he smarmy, Georgie Snood. No wonder I can't stand him.

'Don't you ever come down the sties again, either of you,' Solly Thompson said ever so fierce, 'or I'll feed you to my pigs.'

'I never told him to go down there, Sir,' Georgie Snood said, the lying Toe Rag! 'He run down there before I could stop him. I was just about to shout him to come back when you come out of that sty.'

Well, I don't know why Solly Pig is so upset about it. All that's down in the sties are pigs and pig muck.

Anyway the gas leak was down in the cellar, and like he always does Georgie Snood sent me down to find it. All the Fitters does that, you know, sends the Mates down to find any leaks. Because they say that we're less valuable than they are because we're only trainees and they're fully qualified. So if there's an explosion we'll be less of a loss to the Gas than them.

It was really dark down the cellar and when I told him that I needed a light to see by Georgie Snood said, 'Strike a match then.'

He thinks he's ever so funny, you know.

So just to get him back I shouted up, 'I am striking matches but I still can't see the leak.'

'What? Oh my God!' he yelled. 'You'll blow us all up!' And he went running out of the house.

When I went to look for him he was standing by the garden gate all white-faced and trembly.

'You daft bleeder,' he kept on shouting at me. 'Don't you know no better than to strike matches where there's a leak? You could have blown us all up.'

'But you told me to do it,' I said all innocent and gormless.

Anyway, he gave me a torch then, and I had to go back down and find the leak.

It was dinnertime before we got it mended, and Mrs Thompson had come home and was in the kitchen. She's fat and greasy-looking like her husband, but Georgie Snood was smarming up to her like he does with all the women. He thinks he's a real lady-killer, you know, even though he's got bad teeth and he's ugly.

She had a big iron cooking pot on the

stove and it didn't smell very nice because it was full of pigswill.

'I reckon we made your husband angry this morning, Madam,' Georgie Snood told her. 'He was really upset because my Mate went down to the pigsties to look for him—'

'Oh, was he now.' She looked as if she was going to get mad. 'What was he doing when you found him?'

'He was in a sty with one of the pigs. But I don't know what he was doing because I never saw inside,' I told her. 'But the pig wasn't half squealing.'

'Oh, was it.' She was starting to look mad now.

'Mr Thompson must have been working hard though, because he was ever so red and sweaty when he come out.'

I thought that would cheer her up to know that her husband had been working so hard, but it never though. She just looked really mad, and her face went all tight and hard.

Solly Thompson come in then and asked her, 'Where's me dinner? Have you got it ready?'

'Oh yes,' she said. 'You sit down and I'll bring it to you.'

You'll never believe what she did then! She got a plate and filled it with pigswill from the pot and put it on the table in front of Solly Thompson.

He stared at it like he was seeing things. 'What's this?'

'I was cooking it for your girlfriend,' she told him. 'I thought you might like to have the same as her. And here's your pudding as well.'

She picked up the cooking pot and emptied the swill all over his head, and he just sat there with his mouth wide open.

Georgie Snood run out of the house and I went after him.

'What did she do that for?' I asked him.

'You're gormless, you are,' he said to me. 'Can't you put two and two together yet?'

'Yeah, two and two makes four,' I told him. 'There's no flies on me, Georgie.'

'There's more flies on you than on twenty strips of fly-paper, Specs,' he told me, and went home for his dinner.

Another reason why I don't like mating Georgie Snood is that he gives me all the mucky bits to do, like yesterday when we had to go and do a job at the Rag and Bone Yard down town.

The Rag and Bone man is called Old Charlie, and he's got a wife named Daisy and a son called Filthy Cyril. They don't half stink, all three of them. They never wash themselves or change any of their clothes, they're walking rubbish tips.

Johnny Merry reckons that Old Charlie's got a lot more sons and daughters besides Filthy Cyril, but he says nobody ever sees them because they live in hidden caves under the piles of rubbish in the yard and they only come up on the surface once a month after dark. He says that you can always tell the night when they've come up on the surface because the next morning every fly in the town is laying dead.

In the war Old Charlie, Daisy and Filthy Cyril used to go round town with a big old pram to collect the rags and bones, and when Old Charlie used to get tired he used to sit in the pram and make Daisy push him around. But now he's bought the Co-op horse and cart, because the Co-op has got a new electric van. So the three of them sits in a row on the cart seat and the poor old horse has to drag them round the town. I feel really sorry for that horse.

It can hardly move, it's so old and feeble. Johnny Merry says that it's nine years older than God!

But Old Charlie and Filthy Cyril are very kind to it. When they comes to a hill they makes Daisy get off the cart and help the horse pull it up the hill. Daisy's only small and skinny, but she's ever so strong. Johnny Merry said that a bloke told him that before Daisy got married to Old Charlie she used to be a hod-carrier for a gang of bricklayers. He says that Daisy was known as the 'Fastest Hod in the Midlands'.

Old Charlie's Rag and Bone Yard is really hard to walk around, because it's like one massive mountain of rubbish with narrow passages and dark tunnels going through it. It's like one of those ancient mazes and you can get lost ever so easy in it.

Johnny Merry says that one day some Gyppos came to the yard to sell Old Charlie some scrap iron, and they got lost in the tunnels and were never seen again. He says that for the first couple of weeks that the Gyppos were lost you could sometimes hear them calling for help, but one by one they must have died of starvation because the voices kept on getting weaker and fewer until at last it was all silent. Even I arn't stupid enough to believe that tale. But when I was a little kid I used to believe it when people told me that Old Charlie used to murder people and bury them in the rubbish.

Anyway, when me and Georgie Snood went to the Rag and Bone Yard he stood outside and sent me through the tunnels to find Old Charlie. He lives in a house in the Yard, you know, but you can't tell it's a house because the rubbish covers it up. All you can see of it is a doorway at the end of one of the tunnels, and from outside the Yard you can see a chimney-pot sticking up out of the top of the mountain.

It was a real hot day so the stink was terrible, and the flies was like squadrons of those Japanese kamikazes in the war. They kept on swooping down onto me head and face and buzzing in me ears and biting me. To tell you the truth I nearly give up and run back out, but then I thought of the Foreign Legionnaires marching to Fort Zinderneuf, so I just pretended I was one of them and kept going. I started to imagine what it would be like to get through to Old Charlie's house, and find him and Daisy and Filthy Cyril propped up in the windows and doors like those dead Legionnaires at Fort Zinderneuf. I know it might sound a bit cruel, but I really started to wish that it would happen because then I'd have a real adventure to tell people about, wouldn't I.

Well, after what seemed ever such a long time I got to the house door and when I looked inside there was old rags and bones all over the place, and the gaslight was lit because it was so dark inside the room. They haven't had the electric put in, you see. Old Charlie, Daisy and Filthy Cyril was sitting on orange boxes round the table, eating fish and chips out of a newspaper. When I looked a bit closer I saw that the table was orange boxes as well. The smell was so bad that I had to breathe through me mouth.

'You from the Gas?' Old Charlie looked ever so fierce at me. At least I think he looked fierce, but his face was so dirty and stubbily and he had his cap pulled down so low on his head, I couldn't really see how he was looking.

'Yeah,' I told him.

'I wants that stove shifting.' Old Charlie pointed to the corner, and there was one of those really old gas stoves there only it was hard to recognise what it was because it was so thick in muck and grease. 'It's got to be moved to the other corner there.'

'Right, I'll go and get the Fitter,' I told him, and I run out of there and through the tunnels like a bat out of hell to get out of that stink.

When I told Georgie Snood what had got to be done, he just said, 'Alright then. Get on with it.'

'What? By meself?' I can't take this in.

'It's a simple little job. Just measure how much lead pipe you needs, and blow a couple of fresh joints. That's all it needs.'

'But it stinks in there,' I told him. 'It's making me feel real bad.'

'Phooo.' He snorted all contemptuous. 'Youm bloody kettle-stomached, you am, Specs. A bit of stink won't kill you.'

'Well, it won't kill you either then, will it,' I said.

'There's an emergency job come up while you was inside,' he told me. 'Henry Thrall has sent a message to me that I've got to go and do it straight away, and that you've got to do this little job here by yourself. Henry Thrall says it's time you did a couple of simple jobs by yourself.'

I could tell that he was telling lies. The rotten Toe Rag.

'I'm not going back in there on me own,' I told him.

'Alright then.' He got mad then. 'I'm going to go and tell Henry Thrall that you're refusing to work, and he'll sack you. Your Mam 'ull be pleased to hear that you've been sacked for being lazy, won't she just.'

Won't she just!!!! She'll go stark raving bonkers if I get the sack. God knows what she'll do to me!!!

I still think he's telling lies, mind you.

But, what if he's telling the truth?

'Right then,' he said, and he sounded all confident. 'I'll pop into the yard on me way to the emergency job and tell Henry Thrall that you're refusing to work. It's your own fault, Specs, so don't blame me when he sacks you.'

He started to walk off, and I lost me bottle then.

'Alright. I'll do it on me own.'

I felt as sick as a parrot giving in like that. But what else could I do? Me Mam 'ud kill me if I'd got the sack.

He gives me all the tools and piping and stuff that I'll need, and then walks off.

It was horrible doing that job. I got all filthy and smelly with grease and muck, and when I come back out I was itching like mad all over. I started to walk back through the town, but the itching got so bad that I had to stop and scratch. I took me overalls off and shook them in case there was any fleas on them. And just when I was scratching and shaking Glenda Shortway come out with another girl from the place they worked in and walked past me.

'My God, Glenda,' the other girl said all hoity-toity. 'Where's that awful smell coming from?'

And then they both looked at me, and held their noses.

I was as sick as a parrot, I'll tell you. I don't reckon that Glenda Shortway will ever be my girlfriend now, you know ...

Six

I'm still wearing me old blue double-breasted suit for best, you know. Only it's even worse now because me Mam washed it, and the trousers and sleeves shrunk so they'm nearly halfway up me arms and legs.

But I've decided now that it's more important to be big and have big muscles than to wear a gaberdine drape suit, so I've started a 'Charles Atlas' course. Have you seen the adverts for it in the papers? Charles Atlas is the world's most perfectly developed man. And he got like that because of 'Dynamic Tension'.

You have to send the money and then Charles Atlas sends you the different parts of the 'Dynamic Tension' course every week. And he writes to you as well and asks you to let him know how well you're developing. You have to send him your measurements so that he can see if you're doing the exercises the right way. He says in his letters that in two weeks you'll see the difference in your muscles if you do the exercises every day like he does. If you can't see any difference that's because you're not doing it properly.

The only trouble is I have to hide the letters and instructions, and do my exercises in secret because me Mam 'ull go mad if she finds out I'm spending such a lot of money.

I reckon that must be the reason that so far I'm not growing any muscles. Because I have to keep stopping when she comes upstairs to see what I'm doing.

The thing is, you see, me Mam says that I ought to be saving me money and giving it to her to keep for me. But I don't want to do that again, because Johnny Merry was right when he said that she'd spent the last lot I give her to save for me. So what I tell her is that I haven't got any money to save because I have to buy tools for me job. When she wants to see the tools I'm supposed to have bought I sneak some out of Georgie Snood's toolbag and bring them home to show her. Then sneak them back into the bag again next morning.

She keeps on saying that I should keep the tools at home, but I tell her that we have to keep them at the works because that's the regulations, and when we become Fitters then the Gas will give us all the money back we spent on the tools. I tell her that I'll give her all the money then. But by then I'll be in the Foreign Legion, won't I. That'll shoot her up the backside, won't it.

It's funny you know, but I don't think me Mam loves me at all. All she does is nag me all the time, even when I've done nothing to upset her. I get ever so fed up with it. She keeps on staring at me all angry and then telling me, 'I'm bloody sure that there was a mix-up at the hospital. I can't believe that you're my kid.'

'Oh come now, Effie,' me Dad said last time she told me that. 'Specs is the spitting image of me when I was his age.'

'Oh, is he now,' she said all sneery. 'Well, let me tell you, Horace Kensal, it's a bloody wise child that knows his own father, but a bloody sight wiser father that knows his own child.'

'Har har har, that's a good 'un, Effie,' Sid pipes up.

'And you can shurrup as well, Sidney Tompkin, because I'll bet you got no idea at all who your father was,' she told him all snotty, and he went all sulky and huffy then.

Anyway, this week Charles Atlas sent me the instructions on how to build a wedge-shaped, power-packed torso. That's what he says, a wedge-shaped, power-packed torso. And there was a photo of him on one of the pages showing his torso. It don't half look good. I bet when my torso is wedge-shaped and power-packed all the girls will want to have me for their boyfriend.

I reckon Glenda Shortway will really get jealous when she sees that all the other girls want me. I might let her be my girlfriend, but I'll have to wait and see who else is on offer first, because I saw a girl last week down town who was really beautiful with long black hair and dark eyes. I've never seen her before, and none of the gang knows who she is. She saw me looking at her, but then she just turned her nose up and ignored me. So I'll have to wait until I've finished my Dynamic Tension course before she'll look back at me, I reckon.

Me and Charles Atlas are getting to be good friends as well. In his letters he calls me 'Buddy'. And he's told me that as a favour because I'm his buddy he'll send me an extra course telling me what I've got to eat and drink to develop 'Super Human Action Energy'. And he'll only charge me half price for it. He says in his letter that he can only offer this extra course to men like me who are making such rapid progress with their 'Dynamic Tension'. He says that only one in a hundred do as well as me.

To tell the truth, I cheated a bit when I sent him my 'Muscle and Strength Increase Report' the week before last. I said I'd increased all me measurements by two inches, and he sent back a letter to tell me: 'Congratulations, Buddy! You're one of my All Time Star Students.' And he said he was going to put my name on the 'Roll of Honour'. He said as well that he'd like to have some photos of me, before and after I started the course, and he was going to put them in the magazine. I've got to pay some extra for the cost of doing that but he said that the publicity I'll get with me photos will most probably get me offers of work in the pictures in Hollywood.

Oh yeah, I never explained about the magazine, did I. There's a Charles Atlas magazine comes out every month about 'Dynamic Tension' and for his students it's a special price. So I'm going to have that as well, because as soon as my muscles grow a bit I shall send him the photos he wants. I'm really looking forwards to seeing meself in his magazine. It won't half make the other lads jealous. Especially Johnny Merry.

I've told him about the Dynamic Tension I'm doing, and I said he could share my course with me if he wanted. But he only said that he'd wait and see how big my muscles got before he tried it. He reckons to be a gangster in America you don't need big muscles, only a tommy-gun and a pistol.

We went to see a gangster picture last Sunday. It was really good. All about a gangster named 'Pretty Boy Romano' who kept on saying, 'I'm gonna live fast, die young, and have a good-looking corpse!' That sounds real Big Time City Slicker, don't it. Me and Johnny kept on saying it all the way home.

The pictures are always full on Friday, Saturday and Sunday nights. There's three different lots of seats. The seats in front are one shilling and threepence, the middle are one and ninepence and the circle at the back is two and threepence. All the posh sort of people sit in the circle, and all the courting couples tries to get in the back row of the one and ninepences.

Johnny Merry says that the back row is like a Knocking Shop, the things the courting couples gets up to there. When we're in the mood for some devilment we takes a torch with us and we waits until we knows that the courting couples are getting all hot and steamy and then we walks up to the side of the back row and shines the torch down it, and shouts really loud.

'This is the management speaking. Will that couple in the middle there kindly stop that disgusting behaviour.'

There's always a roar of laughing then from everybody else, and sometimes the girl screams and the bloke shouts and goes mad and tries to get at us. Only when he starts to try and rush along the row he keeps on stamping on people's feet and knocking their legs and there's always somebody who starts fighting with him for doing that. Then we switch the torch off and sneak back in the dark to our own seats before the Manager comes to see what's happening.

The one and threepences are for the younger kids and the roughs and scruffs, and them people who can't see very well and has to sit close to the screen.

Now our gang is at work we always goes in the one and ninepences. All except Fatty Polson, his Mam and Dad still makes him go to the pictures with them and they always sits in the very front row in the one and threepences. Johnny Merry says that by rights the Polsons should be charged double money because they're so fat that they takes up the whole of the front row. They can't sit anywhere else because they can't squeeze in between the rows of seats. Mrs Polson tried to sit further back one night, and she got stuck, and the manager had to send for the Fire Brigade to get her out.

The film that night was *Gone with the Wind.*

All our gang was there and we didn't half laugh because Mrs Polson was stuck so tight she kept on farting ever so loud. You could hear her all over the place, and every time she farted Johnny Merry shouted, 'That's another one gone with the wind! Get her out quick before we're all gone.'

The first fireman who come in got his axe out and started chopping at the seats to free her, and the Manager went mad and tried to stop him and take his axe off him, and they started fighting over the axe.

Then the people started stamping their feet and shouting and there was an uproar. In the end they stopped the film and everybody had to be given their money back. The manager told Mrs Polson that she was barred for life from his picture house. She had to wait until he left and a new manager came who didn't know her before she was able to get in again.

The pictures is one of the places that the girls and lads tries to click with each other, you know. What happens is that if a girl sees a lad she fancies, her and her mate will always wait until the interval when the lights come on, then they'll get up and go arm in arm to the lavatory. They always goes to the lavatory that's furthest away from their seat to give the lad time to see them, and then they'll come back straight away and walk up and down the aisle calling and waving to their other mates but all the time the one girl keeps on staring across at the lad she fancies. If she thinks that she's clicked she'll send her friend then to ask the lad what his name is, and to ask him if he fancies the one who fancies him. If he says yes, then his friend and her friend swop places so that they can sit together. The lads do the same thing.

I've done it meself a few times. But I don't do it anymore because whenever I send one of my mates to ask a girl if she fancies me, she always tells him 'No!'

There was one Sunday night that a girl kept on walking up and down and staring straight at me, and I thought I'd really clicked, but then her friend come and told me ever so snotty, 'Marcia's not looking at you! She's looking at the lad sitting further along. So just stop staring at us, Four Eyes.'

A lot of the girls walks up and down staring at Johnny Merry, you know. Especially when he's wearing his green gaberdine drape suit and blue brothel-creepers and his green silk tie with the bare woman on it in all different colours. And he's chewing gum like Pretty Boy Romano does.

But he always shouts to them, 'You can look but you can never touch, Honey

Baby. So just keep on moving because I got things to do, and people to see.'

He's a real Big Time City Slicker, Johnny Merry is, you know. A real Cool Cat. His favourite singer is Frankie Lane, and he can sing just like him. One of the songs he likes best is 'Mule Train' and he always sings it when we're coming home after the pictures or the dance. It don't half upset the neighbours. They all comes to the bedroom windows and shouts and cusses at him, but he don't care. He just laughs and puts on his Nick Romano voice and tells them, 'Play it cool, Daddyho. Keep it cool, Big Momma.'

Me Mam used to hate Johnny Merry, but now she don't. I heard her telling Hilda about how good-looking Johnny Merry had got since he left school.

'I'll tell you what, Hilda,' she said. 'I'udden't mind teaching that young sod a few tricks meself.'

'I reckon he might think youm a bit too old for him, Effie,' Hilda told her, a bit sneery like.

But me Mam only laughed.

'There's many a good tune played on an old fiddle, Hilda.'

'Well, I wish you'd tell Harold that,'

Hilda said. 'Because he don't never try to play any sort of tune on me anymore.'

Sid Tompkin and me Dad both hate the sight of Johnny Merry though. It's the only thing that they ever agree on.

'Wait until he has to go into the army,' Sid Tompkin keeps on saying. 'They'll soon knock all that cockiness out of the bugger.'

'You're right there, Sid,' me Dad agrees. 'They tames lions in the army. Never mind snot-nosed tearaways like that bugger.'

But when either of them meets him they always falses around him.

'How do, Johnny.'

'How's it going, Kid?'

'My oath, Johnny, you reminds me of how I was when I was a lad.'

'I used to be a real tearaway like you, Johnny.'

Do you know something, I can't help wishing that me Dad was like 'Beau Geste', or 'Beau Sabreur'. Or even Sid was like them. I wish that me Mam could be like one of those Ladies that I read about. It 'ud be great to have somebody from your own family to admire and look up to, wouldn't it ... Instead of what I've got ...

Seven

Aubrey Jones-Evans is back home again. I saw him the other day walking down the street and I said ever so friendly, 'Hiya, Aubrey.'

He just looked at me like I was a piece of dog muck, and said, 'Do I know you?'

'Yeah, I'm Specs.'

'Is that so,' he said, and stuck his nose in the air and went on past.

He was dressed all posh, and I was in me Gas overalls so I expect he didn't want to be seen talking to a scruff in the street. Stuck-up Prat!

He's away at some College or other, and when he's home he wears a blazer with gold buttons, and one of them long scarfs with stripes on wrapped round his neck. He's got ever so tall and lanky as well, he's a lot taller than any of our gang.

Aubrey's Mam and Dad lives in the big house at the top of our street. They're named Idris and Sybil, and they're ever so rich and stuck-up. They hates all of us roughs and scruffs. Sid Tompkin always calls them 'Jumped-up Taffy pit props'. And he says that when they first come to live in England they used to keep their coal in the bath. Mind you, they must be posh to have a bath fixed in the house, because nobody else in our street has got one. We have to use the tin bath in front of the fire once a week.

There's another big house in our street with a lot of trees round it and a massive big garden and in the war it was a Hostel for girls who came to work in the factories round here. We still calls it the Hostel, but now it's used by the Council as offices. That used to have baths fixed in it as well, but I don't know if it's still got them now it's been changed to offices.

Me and Johnny Merry was queueing in the shop last Tuesday to buy some bacon for me dinner, and Mrs Jones-Evans was in there wearing her new fur coat and a big hat with feathers in it and the shopman said to her, 'Saw your son yesterday, Madam. What a fine young man he is, as well. Looking like a real young gentleman. A bit different from the other young scruffs hereabouts, aren't he.'

The silly cow preened herself like a peacock.

'It's his good breeding, Mr Brant,' she told him. 'It's in the blood, you know. Our blood lines ensure that the Jones-Evans menfolk all grow tall and distinguished. Such a contrast to the poor underpriviliged people around us. They're rather dwarf-like, aren't they?'

Johnny Merry pretended to be all puzzled. 'What happened to your old man then, Missus? Didn't he get his transfusion? Because he's only a short-arse, aren't he. Mind you, I expect when he was down the coal mine holding up the roof the weight of it must have crushed him down until he was shorter than before he went down it.'

'How dare you?' She went mental! 'How dare you talk about your betters in such a rude manner.'

'It's the only way us poor underpriviliged dwarfs knows how to talk, Missus,' Johnny teased her.

'If my son Aubrey was here, he'd give you a damm good thrashing for your impudence,' she told him, and under the paint her face was all mottled and purply.

'Give me a thrashing, that bloody giraffe

you got? He couldn't give my Granny a thrashing.'

Johnny aren't scared of nobody, you know. Least of all lanky Aubrey.

'You ought to keep him tied up, Missus, because if he keeps on walking round with his nose in the air he's going to trip over a lamppost.'

The people in the queue started to laugh and Mrs Jones-Evans went storming out without buying anything, and the shopman laughed with the rest of us, and said, 'She's a silly stuck-up mare, aren't she.'

But I reckon he's two-faced himself, crawling to her face and saying that behind her back.

Do you know, when I was a kid I couldn't understand why people was so two-faced, and now I'm not a kid, I still can't understand why people are so two-faced.

Look at all the blokes on the Gas. They goes to people's houses and are nice as pie to their faces and if it's a posh house they acts all humble, but when nobody's in the house they pokes around in all the drawers and cupboards to see what's there. They don't pinch anything, but I still don't think it's right. They shouldn't go poking into people's private things, should they. And then afterwards they takes the mickey out of the people's things.

Georgie Snood is always doing that. He stands there with his cap in his hand going, 'Yes Sir, no Sir, three bags full, Sir.' And the minute the people go out he calls them a load of wankers, and he's rummaging around all over the place, pulling underclothes and that out of the drawers and saying, 'Look at this, Specs. This woman who lives here must be a right tart. If I caught my missus wearing this I'd knock her into the middle of next week.'

He's always going on about knocking people into the middle of next week, but the only one he tries to do that to is me, whenever I makes him mad, which is usually about six times a day. It's a good job I'm quick on my feet, or I'd be spending half my life living in the future.

Another thing I don't like about him is the way he keeps on talking about sex all the time. Every time there's a young woman in the house he keeps on poking me in the ribs and whispering, 'God, I'd like to shag her. I 'udden't half make her squeal. I'd give her a real good seeing to.'

And he keeps on asking me, 'Has you had a shag yet, Specs? I'd had dozens of shags when I was your age. I was shagging every night, I was.'

It makes me feel uncomfortable when an old man like him talks like that. I mean, me and the gang tell dirty jokes sometimes and look at dirty pictures, but we're young, aren't we, and anyway we don't keep on talking about it all the time. And I've never done it with a girl, or anybody else. I think about it a lot, but I've never done it. Johnny Merry says he's done it lots of times. He says he knows a girl down town who does it all the time, and if I like he'll take me down to see her and she'll let me do it as well. I should like to try it, but to tell you the truth, I'm a bit scared of doing it.

I had a good laugh one day with Georgie Snood though. It was a real hot day and we went to do a job fixing a pipe up the side of the kitchen wall at a big posh house, and there was a posh woman in the garden who was doing some weeding and every time she bent over her skirt went up at the back. Georgie Snood was up the ladder and he kept on craning his neck to watch her bending over, and he was getting so excited that he craned his neck so far that he fell off the ladder and into the water barrel underneath.

He went in headfirst and his legs was kicking, and I was laughing so much I couldn't pull him out. He nearly drowned, but then a bloke came and got him out, and Georgie Snood sat blowing water out of his mouth and cussing and swearing like a maniac. Then he come after me with the hammer because he reckoned I'd pushed the ladder on purpose to tip him off. But I hadn't, not really. But thinking about it now, I wish I had.

Do you know what I did the other day? I wrote a letter to the French Embassy in London. Yeah! Really! I did. I asked them if they could pay for me to go to France and join the Foreign Legion. I've read every book that the library has got about the Foreign Legion. There's some good books about it written by a man named P C Wren. *Beau Geste. Beau Sabreur. Sinbad the Soldier.* They're brilliant!

If the French Embassy says that they'll pay my fares, then I'll only have to save up enough money to get me passport. The trouble is that me Mam or Dad will have to sign the form for me when I send for me passport, because I'm too young to get one without their permission. I don't think they'll sign it for me though. Johnny Merry says that he'll sign it for me and use me Dad's name on it. But you can get sent to prison for doing that, can't you. I don't think I'd like to go to prison. It's alright for Johnny because he's already been in a boy's prison, hasn't he. So he's used to it. He says it's nothing. He says that he could do any sentence sitting on his pot. The pot is the pisspot they give to convicts when they go into their cells. Anyway it's no good worrying about it yet. Not until I get a letter from the French Embassy.

I know a couple of blokes who've been to men's prisons. The one bloke is called 'Digger', because he was digging rocks in Dartmoor for years. He arn't half tough! But funny enough he's always nice to me when he sees me. I asked him one day what he'd got sent to Dartmoor for, and he laughed and told me, 'Armed robbery from a gas meter, Specs.'

Then another time he told me, 'I got seven years' hard labour for committing grievous bodily harm on a midget. The odds were ten men to one that night, and he was the toughest midget our gang had ever had a fight with, he knocked nine of us unconscious and left me laying bleeding.'

Now what was I telling you about before? Oh yeah. Aubrey Jones-Evans. Mrs Jones-Evans didn't half make me Mam mad one day a few weeks ago. They was both in the Post Office down town and me Mam said hello to her, and trying to be friendly asked her when Aubrey was coming home from college.

'In a month's time,' Mrs Jones-Evans told her, and me Mam said, 'Well, if he gets lonely he can go to the pictures with our Specs.'

She says Mrs Jones-Evans looked down her nose at her and said all snotty-like, 'Specs? Specs? Oh, isn't that the scruffy boy who wears spectacles and looks mentally retarded? Oh no, I don't think my Aubrey would enjoy his company, thank you.'

And before me Mam could think of anything to say back, Mrs Jones-Evans buggered off out of the post office.

You should have heard me Mam carrying on about her when she come back home. The air was blue!

I was mad with me Mam though. Who does she think I am? I don't want to go to the pictures with a stuck-up prat like Aubrey Jones-Evans, thank you ...

Eight

I saw that girl with the long black hair again today. I was going back to the Gasworks to get some stuff for Georgie Snood and I had to pass down the poshest street in the town. It's called Old Mill Avenue and it's all big houses and gardens and every house has got a garage and some of them has even got tennis courts. Sometimes we have to go and do jobs there, and when we do, Henry Thrall the Boss always tells the Fitter who's going to do the job:

'Make sure you've got a clean shirt and overalls on, and do a good job, or else.'

They don't like to see us roughs and scruffs down there, I can tell you. Whenever me and the gang goes along it you can see the curtains twitching and as sure as God made little apples there's a copper comes along on his bike before we even get to the end of the avenue.

Anyway, I was riding my bike and I went to pass one of the tennis court houses and just as I went past it a tennis ball came bouncing out across the road. So I stopped and picked it up. Then somebody shouted, 'Will you throw the ball back, please?'

Me heart started to thump ever so hard, and I felt like I'd got a big lump in me throat. It was the girl with the long black hair. She was wearing a little white blouse and a little white skirt and she looked beautiful, just like a film star. Her face was all suntanned and her arms and legs were all nice and brown as well. I couldn't help staring at her, and she laughed, and her teeth were all lovely and white.

'Can I have my ball back, please?'

To tell the truth I'd forgot I was holding it. I felt ever such a dummy, and I threw the ball back, but it hit the wire netting fence and bounced back at me, and she laughed again, and I could feel meself going all red.

'Is there a problem, Sophia?' This bloke shouted then, and he come to stand by her inside the fence. He was wearing a white shirt and shorts as well, and when

I picked the ball up and went to chuck it over again I saw who it was. Aubrey Jones-Evans! That stuck-up prat!

It was such a shock that I missed me aim, and the ball bounced off and come back again.

'Oh God!' He acted all disgusted. 'Can't you throw a ball accurately?'

He was looking at me as if I was a bit of dog-dirt and making out that he didn't know me from Adam, so I was just about to give him a right mouthful, and then I looked at the girl with the long black hair again, and I didn't want to swear in front of her, so I didn't say nothing.

She told that prat all sharp, 'Oh, do be quiet, Aubrey. He's doing his best.'

I was really careful this time and the ball sailed over into the court, and he run after it, but she stayed and smiled at me.

'Thank you very much.'

She was looking at me as if she was waiting for me to say something, but I couldn't think of anything to say. It was like me tongue was glued inside me mouth.

Then she waved and run off laughing, but it wasn't like nasty laughing so I didn't mind.

I wanted to stay and watch her play tennis, but I felt all funny about doing that, so I just went on to the Gasworks.

All the way there I was practising saying her name, 'Sophia'. I reckon it's a lovely name that. 'Sophia, Sophia, Sophia.'

I was thinking how good it would be if she was my girlfriend. We could get married, and go shopping together every Saturday afternoon, and go to the Memorial Hall dance on Saturday nights and to the pictures on Sunday nights. Of course, if we got married I wouldn't be able to join the Foreign Legion. But I'd sooner be married to Sophia than go marching over the desert to get killed at Fort Zinderneuf.

Trouble was, when I got back to the Gasworks I couldn't remember all the things that Georgie Snood had sent me to get for the job we was doing.

Herbert Taylor, the boss storeman, is a miserable sod and he stood tapping his foot and telling the rest of the blokes in the stores, 'Bloody kids today, they'm bloody useless. No good for nothing. I don't know what the world is coming to, I really don't. I wouldn't pay this lot in bloody washers.'

Old Billy, who's the stores labourer, just grinned and winked at me. He's a good bloke, Old Billy is. He's an old soldier, you know, and he's got medals from both wars. He's seen more action than all the rest of the blokes on the Gas put together. He got badly wounded just before the war finished and his lungs are all shot up, so he has trouble breathing and has to move a bit slow. Herbert Taylor gives him a rough time, always nagging at him and shouting, and I said to Old Billy one day, 'Why do you put up with that miserable sod shouting at you, Billy? When you've got all those medals?'

He just grinned and told me, 'Medals don't count for nothing in this life, Specs, not when the fighting's all over and done with. While I was out fighting in the wars the buggers like Herbert Taylor were sitting on their arses back here at home making sure that they'd get all the cushy jobs when the war was over. So when I come back I'd got nothing except me demob suit, and the Royal Standbacks like Taylor was well set up for life.'

It's a funny thing about the Fitters, you know, but none of them went to fight in the war. They was all in the 'Royal

Standbacks', I reckon.

I asked Georgie Snood one day why he hadn't been in the Forces when the war was on, and he told me, 'I volunteered for the Commandos, and they was very keen to have me as well, but when Henry Thrall found out that I was going to go into the Commandos he went bloody mad about it, and said he wouldn't let me leave the Gas on no account. He said that without me being here this department would just fall to pieces. So I had to stay at home instead of going for a Commando. I wasn't half disappointed though, I can tell you.'

Nearly all the Fitters comes out with stories like that when you ask them why they wasn't in the War.

I was telling me Mam about them one day, and Sid said all sneery, 'Them bloody Fitters all sounds like a load of bloody War-Dodgers to me.'

'Well, if anybody should know what they am, it's you, Sidney Tompkin,' me Mam told him.

'What do you mean, Effie? I should know if anybody should?' he asked her, and she said all sweet, 'Well, it's like the old saying, aren't it, Sidney. It takes one to know one.'

He went all red then, and shouted, 'My God! My God! I suffered summat awful fighting for my King and Country, but I'm suffering worse now because I'm not allowed to talk about what I did in the war. But just you wait, Effie Kensal, the day will come when you'll go down on your knees to beg my forgiveness for having doubted me all these years. Just you wait until I gets that letter releasing me from the Official Secrets Act, then you'll be sorry.'

Anyway, never mind Sid now, I just can't understand how Old Billy stops himself from clouting Herbert Taylor sometimes. I mean, he's been in all them battles in both the wars so he must be tough. But when I asked him why he didn't clout Taylor he just shook his head and said all serious, 'I need this job, Specs. Like I told you, medals don't count for nothing in peacetime. With me being buggered up in me lungs there's not many employers who'll give me work.'

'Well, I shouldn't put up with it if I'd been in the army like you have,' I told him. 'I'd give him a smack in the chops.'

But he only chuckled. 'You'll learn, Specs. You'll learn.'

Do you know, I thought that when I left

school and started work I should know a lot more about everything than I does. But life just seems to get harder to understand the older I gets.

Anyway, because I can't remember what Georgie Snood sent me to get, Herbert Taylor tells me, 'I can't waste any more time with you if you can't remember what you've been sent for. So bugger off back and ask Georgie Snood to write it down for you next time, you bloody thick-yedded young bugger.'

So I rode back to the job, and I was feeling a bit scared of what Georgie Snood might do. When I went down Old Mill Avenue I stopped by the house where I'd seen Sophia because I wanted to look at her again, and I was hoping that the ball would come over the fence so that I could see her smile at me when I threw it back for her. But the tennis court was empty, and I felt really disappointed.

By the time I got back to the job I was feeling down in the mouth and fed up with everything.

Georgie Snood went mad at me for not bringing the stuff back and he cussed and swore at me until he was frothing in the mouth. Then he clouted me real hard across my earhole, and it was ever so strange because it hurt ever so bad and me head started spinning and I suddenly saw Sophia's face rise up in front of me, and then in me head I could hear Herbert Taylor swearing and shouting at Old Billy and when Georgie Snood clouted me again I suddenly lost me temper and I must have hit him back.

I couldn't believe it! He went flying over onto his arse, and he sat there staring up at me and his eyes was bulging out of his head, and I thought he'd jump up and kill me, but he'd gone all white and I suddenly thought:

'He's scared of me!'

I couldn't believe it!

But when he just kept sitting staring bulgy-eyed and rubbing his jaw, I started to know that it was true. He was scared of me! The big bully was scared!

I felt sorry for what I'd done then and I went to help him up. But he kept scrabbling backwards on his arse and skreeking, 'Keep away, you bloody maniac or I'll have the law on you. Keep away from me! Help, Police! Help! Help, Police!'

The woman whose house we was in

come running to see what all the noise was about, and when he saw her Georgie Snood shouted, 'Don't go near him, Missus. He's a mad dog! Fetch the police! He's trying to kill me! For God's sake fetch the police!'

She screamed and run out of the house shouting, 'Help! Murder! Police!'

And I got really scared then, and I run out of the house and jumped on my bike and pedalled away as fast as I could.

The trouble was that it didn't seem to matter how fast I pedalled and how far I got along the road, I couldn't stop being scared of what was going to happen to me. I thought, if the police get me then I'll go to jail for years and years.

So then I thought, why not run away now and join the Foreign Legion? I could pedal down to the coast and stow away on a ship to France. I could tell the French that I'd lost me passport overboard, but that me Main was sending me another one through the post to Paris.

As soon as I thought about going now to join the Foreign Legion I didn't half cheer up quick. I should be just like Beau Geste, shouldn't I. Wrongly accused of doing something I hadn't done. Acting like a true English Gentleman to save my family's name from being disgraced.

Well, I know that I clouted Georgie Snood but it was his own fault really, wasn't it. He'd kept on hitting me first, hadn't he. I'd only give him a bit of his own medicine back, hadn't I.

And when I get killed in Fort Zinderneuf everybody back here at home will be really sorry, and they'll say, 'Beau Specs. Gallant Gentleman.'

And at my funeral there'll be a bugler sounding the Last Post, and hundreds and hundreds of Foreign Legionnaires all presenting arms, and they'll all have tears in their eyes, and all the Foreign Legion Generals will be saluting with their swords, and on the horizon there'll be all these Tuareg warriors on stallions, thousands and thousands of them, who've come to pay their respects and say farewell to 'Beau Specs', their noble enemy who had single-handedly beaten them back from the walls of Fort Zinderneuf before he got killed just as the Relief Column came marching up from Fort Tokotu.

And Sophia will come to my funeral and she'll be wearing a long dress and a black veil, and she'll be weeping as she puts a single red rose on my coffin. And

Glenda Shortway will be there as well, and she'll be wearing a long dress and a black veil and she'll put a single red rose on my coffin. And Johnny Merry and the rest of our gang will be there, and they'll all be telling everybody about what a great bloke I was. And all the Gas Fitters will be there, telling everybody how sorry they are for being so nasty to me, and how wonderful they think I am now. And me Mam and Sid and me Dad and Virgy will all be there, and all the neighbours, and they'll all be crying and saying that they wished they had been nicer to me. And Uncle Harold will be there wearing his top hat and tailcoat, and Hilda will be there dressed in all them black veils like she's the Spirit of Death welcoming me into Valhalla ...

Then I had a puncture!

It was in me back wheel, as well. The worst one to get at. And I hadn't got a puncture outfit neither.

Don't I have rotten luck! How can I get to France when me back tyre's got a puncture in it?

Well, I started to push me bike along the road, and I hadn't gone very far when I heard a voice shouting me from back along the road.

You'll never guess who it was. It was Georgie Snood!

I looked back at him, and he was coming haring along on his bike, and I thought, 'Oh yeah, he's coming to beat me up for hitting him back like I did.'

Well, I got to admit I felt a bit nervous then. Because he's a lot bigger than me, you know. But I thought of my secret name, 'Beau Specs', and of Fort Zinderneuf, and I thought, 'Alright then, Beau. This is it! The Legion's Last Stand!'

And I was feeling okay about it, apart from being scared, I mean.

So I put me bike down on the side on the road and I waited for him.

When he got to me all he said was, 'I never thought that you couldn't take a joke, Specs. I'm really disappointed in you. I was only having a bit of fun with you, there was no need for you to run off like that.'

I can't take this in, you know. He's all smiling and everything. Mind you, the smile looks a bit false to me.

'What's happened to your bike? Why

was you pushing it?' he wanted to know.

'I got a puncture in the back wheel.' I showed him.

'Right then. You take my bike and go back to the works. This is the stuff I wants you to get for me.'

He handed me his bike and a bit of paper with a list printed on it.

'I'll wheel your bike back to the job, and you can sort it out when we'se finished work.'

I can't take this in at all. Why is he being alright with me? Why aren't he being mad with me no more? Why aren't the police with him, and why aren't he telling me that he's going to get me the sack?

'Go on. Get moving,' he told me, and picked up my bike and started wheeling it back along the road we'd come down.

Well, I thought that I might as well go and get the stuff he wanted. Because now I'd got a puncture I couldn't go to France, could I. So until I've got enough money to go and join the Foreign Legion, I might as well stay working on the Gas.

I'll just have to box a bit clever and watch to see what Georgie Snood is up to though. Because I still don't like him at all. And even though he's being as nice as pie to me I know that he don't like me at all neither.

Nine

I clicked last night! Yeah, really! I clicked with a girl last night.

I clicked when me and Fatty Polson was hanging about down town. We'd gone to the youth club first, but it was ever so boring.

Donald Dunmow's cousin was there. His name is Alistair Pickles, and he's in something called the Church of Light Army. He's always dressed up in a brown and purple uniform like the doorman at the Pictures, and he aren't half got a bob on himself. He thinks he's the 'cat's whiskers'.

He's over eighteen years old, you know, so really he ought to have been called up for the real army by now to do his National Service. But Johnny Merry says that Pickles joined the Church of Light

Army to get out of going into the real army. Johnny reckons that Pickles is one of them Conscientious Objectors, like Donald Dunmow is.

Everybody round our way always says that the Conscientious Objectors are just cowards who are too windy to go into battle and fight for their country. You should hear Fatty Polson's dad going on about them. He really hates them, you know. So does Sid and me Dad. And all the blokes on the Gas as well.

I used to believe what they all said about the Objectors. Because I can't understand how any bloke doesn't want to go and have adventures, and being in a war must be a brilliant adventure, mustn't it. But then I started noticing that all the blokes who was ranting and raving the most against the Objectors had never been in any battles themselves. Look at Fatty Polson's dad, for instance. When I was a kid in the war I remember how Fatty Polson's dad was in the army, but he kept on running away from it and coming back home to hide in the coal cellar, and the Redcaps used to come and fetch him back to the army again.

Mrs Masters, whose son Henry was

fighting the Japs in Burma, used to say that Fatty Polson's dad was 'a bleedin' useless lump of fat and would never be a soldier for as long as he'd got a hole in his arse. That the only soldiering he ever did was sweeping out the Naafi in Aldershot'. In fact she still says that about him, even now. So when you think about it, Fatty Polson's dad was as big a coward as any of the Conscientious Objectors, wasn't he.

Anyway, in the end I asked Mr Sambourn what he thought about the Conscientious Objectors. Because Mr Sambourn is a real hero who won medals for bravery in the First War.

I haven't told you about Mr Sambourn before, have I. Well, he's an old bloke who's a real good friend of mine. He lives by himself in one of the old cottages down Herod's Yard. He told me that his missus died a long time ago and he's got a son who lives in America.

Mr Sambourn is ever so interesting to talk to even though he's so old, and he tells me about all sorts of things. I reckon he's the cleverest bloke I've ever met. He went to university and everything and he's been all over the world, and he was in a lot of battles in the First War.

He never brags about anything though, and never says he's been a hero or anything like that. But Frankie Savin told me one day that Mr Sambourn had won medals for bravery in the First War.

Frankie Savin used to live next door to me. He was a paratrooper in the war. His Mam and Dad still lives next door to me, but Frankie's married now and moved away. He's a real good bloke, he was my hero when I was a little kid, and in a way he's still me hero even now. He never bullshitted about what he'd done or hadn't done, and if he tells me that Mr Sambourn was a hero in the First War, then I know it's the truth.

Not like when Sid Tompkin or me Dad tells me anything. If either of them woke me up on Saturday morning and told me that it was Saturday, then the first thing I'd do would be to run outside and ask the first person I saw what day it was.

Anyway, Mr Sambourn told me, 'Specs, beware the man who tries to cover up his own physical cowardice by claiming a moral justification for refusing to risk himself in battle.

'Beware equally the man who tries to cover up his own physical cowardice by vociferously attacking the first type of man.

'For myself personally, Specs, I agree with the immortal Doctor Samuel Johnson, who said, "I like the company of soldiers better than any other type of men", and he said also, "Every man thinks poorly of himself for not having been a soldier".'

To tell you the truth Mr Sambourn just mixed me up with what he said. And he could see that he had, because the next minute he laughed and told me, 'Listen, Specs, Hypocrisy comes in many disguises, and Conscientious Objection can be one of them, as equally can be the strident assertion of Patriotism. But perhaps some of the Objectors, as well as some of the Strident Patriots, are genuine in their beliefs. You must make your own mind up about the individuals you meet.'

Well, it's easy for me to make me own mind up about Donald Dunmow and Alistair Pickles. I think that they're both real Prats. And if they're what Conscientious Objectors are, then I don't want to be one of them.

Our Virgy goes to the club as well and she really fancies Alistair Pickles. Her and her mates reckons he's ever so handsome. They reckons he looks just like Clark Gable in *Gone with the Wind.*

Well, I've seen *Gone with the Wind* and the only way that Alistair Pickles looks like Clark Gable is that he's got the same big, stick-out ears. They're the only things stopping Alistair Pickles' cap falling right down over his face.

The first time Alistair Pickles come to the club Donald Dunmow made us all stand in rows and then he said, 'I want to introduce you to my dear cousin, and Brother in the Lord, Captain Alistair Pickles, who I'm proud to say is the youngest Captain in the Church of Light Army and a veteran of many hard-fought matches against the Devil and his evil minions.'

All the crawlers cheered and clapped then. But our gang just laughed, because Johnny Merry shouted, 'The Devil won the last match ten to one according to the *Sporting Pink,* didn't he, Captain Pickles.'

And Donald Dunmow looked daggers at us, as though we was some of the Devil's evil minions. I like that word, minions, I read it in a book ages ago and looked it up in Uncle Harold's dictionary. I've been trying to use it at work, but everybody there is too thick so I've never had a chance to slip it into any of the talking. I read ever such a lot, you know. I'm really beginning to learn things. I wish now that when I'd been at school I'd paid more attention to what the teachers was telling us. Me Mam hates me reading so much though.

She always grumbles at me, 'What's the good of learning stuff from books when youm Working Class like you am? It only gives you ideas above your station, and makes you all stuck-up and snotty. Anyway, it'll make you go blind sitting with your nose stuck in a book all the time.'

Blimey! That's two things that I like doing that'll make me blind!

I can't take it in, you know, why me Mam keeps on at me all the time. It don't matter what I do, she thinks it's wrong and has a go at me. If I go out with me mates she tells me off for always gallivanting about, and if I stay in she has a go at me for being under her feet. If I read a book she reckons I'm getting ideas above me station, and if I don't do nothing she tells me off for wasting me time day-dreaming. She never has a go at Virgy though. Virgy's her pet.

Did you know that Virgy has gone all religious again? When we was kids Virgy reckoned that she seen the Virgin Mary and Baby Jesus on the old mangle in the backyard and she built a shrine on the mangle and used to pray to it all the time. She was really famous for it. All the neighbours and people from all over the place used to come and watch her praying at her shrine. Then she got tired of all that and was a bit more normal for a long time. But now that she fancies Alistair Pickles she reckons that the Lord has sent her another message, and that she's got to join the Army of the Church of Light. So she's dyed all her clothes brown to make her uniforms, and she's got Uncle Harold's old Home Guard hat and she's dyed that brown as well, and pinned a tin cross on it, and she goes round wearing her uniform and hat all the time, even in the house. She got hold of some big pieces of cardboard and some crayons and she's made a lot of signs which she's pinned up all round the rooms.

They says things like:

'Remember, God is watching you!' and

'Repent, for the Day of Judgement is at hand' and 'Sinners shall be cast into the Pit of Hell. This means You!'

Sid didn't half play up when she put the signs up.

'Jesus Christ Almighty! That daft little cow's gone bloody raving mad again!'

But me Mam jumped straight down his throat. 'You leave my child alone, Sid Tompkin. Or else you'll have me to deal with.'

There's times I feel sorry for Sid, you know. Because since me Dad come back me Mam has treated poor Sid like a lodger, and whenever he has a moan about anything she just tells him real sharp, 'If you don't like living here, Sid Tompkin, you knows where the door is.'

Of course, me Dad saw his chance to get further into me Mam's good books, didn't he. He told Virgy that he was beginning to 'See the Light' himself, and wanted to be 'Washed in the Blood of the Lamb'.

Whenever he has anything to eat now he makes a big show of crossing himself and thanking the Lord for his grub, even if it's just a piece of bread and dripping.

Sid glares daggers at him when he does this, but he daren't say anything snotty about it because he's too scared of what me Mam might do to him if he does.

So he just keeps coming up to me and whispering in me ear, 'Some day, Specs! Some day! You'll see the real Sidney Tompkin.'

I don't know what he means when he says this, because when I ask him he just looks all sort of mysterious and slices his fingers across his throat, then taps the side of his nose, and curls his lip like Humphrey Bogart.

Anyway, last night me and Fatty Polson went to the youth club first and guess what?

Alistair Pickles was there to give a talk about the Church of Light's Missions to the Pygmies in Africa. And Donald Dunmow closes up everything so that everybody has to sit and listen to his cousin, and it's really boring doing that because Alistair Pickles talks 'laaiiike thaaaat youuuuuu knowwwwww', so me and Fatty Polson went down town instead.

We went to watch the television in Curry's windows first, but all that was on was an old bloke's head saying something, and because you can't hear what they say on the televisions in Curry's windows it was a bit boring. So then we went to the Bandstand in the Recreation Gardens, because there's nearly always somebody or other that we knows hanging about there.

The Recreation Gardens. That's the posh name for a bit of waste ground, with a lot of dead bushes, and a fountain which hasn't got any water coming out of it, and a pool that's dry and filled with rubbish and broken bottles, and some rickety old benches that most of the planks has fallen off.

Filthy Cyril and Mad Jack collected all the broken bits together one night, and they made a bonfire in the Recreation Gardens. They was sitting there all happy, but what they hadn't noticed was that they'd made the bonfire too close to the bushes, and suddenly the whole lot went up in flames. Well, it was ever so windy that night and the burning leaves went flying all over the place and was starting fires in people's front yards and shopfronts and the Fire Brigade was called out and all the police come running blowing their whistles and one copper arrested Filthy Cyril and Mad Jack and took them round to the Police Station.

This copper was new in the town, and he was still young and wet behind the ears.

When he got them into the Station the Sergeant behind the desk went mad at him.

'What are you trying to do, you stupid berk?' he was ranting and raving. 'What the Hell has you brought them two round here to my nice clean station for?'

'They was trying to set the town on fire,' the young copper told him.

'Bloody good job too!' the sergeant skreeked.

He comes from Brummagem, you see, and he hates everybody in our town, because he knows that we all hates the Brummies.

'Now take 'um back to where you found 'um,' he tells the young copper, 'and let them get on with the good work.'

So that's why Filthy Cyril and Mad Jack never got sent to prison for trying to burn the town down.

Anyway, when me and Fatty Polson got to the Bandstand last night there was no sign of Filthy Cyril or Mad Jack, but the 'Three Musketeers' was laying sprawled out on the floor of the Bandstand. They was as drunk as lords, and they had a row of milk bottles in front of them, so we knew they'd been drinking Gas Cocktails.

Do you know how to make a Gas Cocktail? It's what Dossers like the Three Musketeers drink when they haven't got enough money to buy a bottle of red wine and Meths to make Red Biddy with.

They goes and pinches bottles of milk from off people's doorsteps and then they bubbles coal gas through the milk. They reckon that when they do that the milk holds all the stuff from the gas and it nearly blows their heads off when they drink it. They says that they gets all the nourishment they needs from it as well, because of the milk. Our gang tried it once, but it tasted so horrible that none of us could manage more than a little sip. Terry Murtagh was bad in bed for a week after his sip as well. So none of us have ever drunk it since.

A lot of people don't like the Three Musketeers, because they say that they're lazy, good for nothing dossers, who won't work. But I like them, because sometimes they really make me laugh, the things they come out with. Mind you, I don't stay with them for very long because sometimes they smell really bad, and other times they're so drunk that they can't even speak, never mind hold a conversation.

They all live together in the woods. They builds camps out of anything that they can scrounge and sometimes the police makes them knock their camps down, and then they sleeps under the bushes, until they can scrounge some stuff to build another camp with.

Ivorski the Pole is the chief musketeer, and his two mates are called Okefonokee and Monkey Balls. Okefonokee is named after that big swamp in America because he can suck down anything, and he looks like a swamp, always covered with mud and dead leaves and stuff like that. Monkey Balls got his name because every time you see him he's shivering like mad, and his teeth are chattering, and he keeps on moaning, 'It's cold enough to freeze the balls off a brass monkey.'

I like Ivorski the Pole best though. Every time somebody says hello to him and asks him how he's doing, he just shakes his head and tells them, 'What a life! What a life! I haven't got enough money to live, and I've got too much money to die.'

'What would you do if you won the

pools?' I asked him one day.

'I'd buy a herd of milking cows and a gasworks, Specs,' he told me, 'and I'd give free Gas Cocktails to every dosser in the world.'

He's very good-natured, you know. When he saw me and Fatty Polson coming round the Bandstand he shouted me to come and have some Gas Cocktail.

At least I think that was what he shouted, only when he stood up he fell down again straight away, so I couldn't hear him properly.

And then I saw Delphine and her mate sitting on the bench by the fountain. Only I didn't know she was called Delphine when I saw her, I found that out later on.

Me and Fatty Polson sat down on another bench and I pretended to be all City Slicker and Cool. I just sat back with me arms over the back of the bench and pretended I was chewing gum like the Yanks does. I had to pretend I was chewing gum, because I hadn't got any fags to smoke, and I hadn't got any gum to chew neither. I kept staring at the fountain, which was a bit boring really, because it never does anything, and it's all rusty so it don't look very nice neither.

Fatty Polson kept on staring at the girls, and they kept giggling and whispering to each other, and after a bit they got up and walked off, but they kept looking back at us, so I knew they fancied me.

No, it wasn't Fatty Polson they fancied, because no girls ever fancies him. He's too fat and ugly. That's one of the reasons I like knocking about with Fatty Polson. He makes me look ever so good-looking when I'm standing next to him. But he don't know that he's ugly, you know. He thinks that a lot of girls fancy him. So he says, 'Let's follow them. I reckon we can click.'

At first I felt a bit nervous about following them, because I've never clicked with a girl before, have I. But then, they turns round and walks back past us, whispering and giggling and looking at us, so this time we follow them. We walk round and round and round the fountain until I'm getting giddy, and then Delphine stops walking and says to me, 'What's you following us for? What does you want?'

I act all City Slicker and cool, and try to think of something good to say to her, but I can't think of anything and then Fatty Polson says, 'Are you talking to me, or am you chewing a brick?'

'No, I'm playing tennis,' Delphine tells him. She's very witty, you see.

'Well, can we play as well?' Fatty Polson says.

'Yes, if you've brought your bat and ball,' Delphine says as quick as lightning.

Everybody goes quiet then, because nobody can think of what to say next. I have a good look at the girls though. Delphine is a bit fat and spotty, but she's alright, but her mate is really fat, so I don't fancy her at all.

'This one 'ull know me the next time he sees me, won't he Jill, the way he's staring at me,' Delphine says to her mate, then tells me, 'Aren't your mam never told you that it's rude to stare?'

'He's staring at you because he fancies you.' Fatty Polson tells her, and I can feel meself going all red, but I still can't think of anything to say.

'Well, she fancies him as well, don't you, Delphine,' her mate says.

'I did a bit, but he's too quiet,' Delphine told her. 'Come on, let's go.'

Then they both just run off, and they didn't turn and look back.

'You prat!' Fatty Polson got all narked

at me. 'We'd clicked there, if only you'd have said summat. Youm bloody hopeless, you am.'

And he just turned and walked away from me as well.

But I didn't care. I was feeling all pleased really. Because that was the first time that a girl had said she fancied me. And although I wouldn't want to get married to Delphine and go shopping with her on Saturday afternoons and to the the pictures on a Sunday, I was still glad that she'd fancied me. So I clicked with her really, didn't I. But I'm still going to join the Foreign Legion. That's unless I can click with Glenda Shortway, or Sophia. If I click with either of them I might stay at home instead ...

Ten

I'll tell you something. Me Dad is embarrassing me, he's really showing me up. He goes down town every day in his big hat with the corks dangling from it and keeps walking round and round the shops saying to everybody he meets:

'Good on you, Cobber. It's fair dinkum today, arn't it. But it's cold enough to freeze the balls off a Kangaroo. So I reckon it's time an old Bwana like meself was heading on back to the campfire. Good Day, Blue.'

Now everybody in the town is calling him 'Didgeridoo', and when some of the kids see him, they start hopping about like kangaroos and shouting, 'Show us your boomerang, Didgeridoo.'

But he's too thick to see that they're taking the mickey and he comes back home and tells us, 'I'll tell you what, this town has never seen anybody like me before. Ned Kelly arn't got nothing on me.'

'I'll say he arn't, Horace Kensal,' Sid always growls at him. 'The way youm robbing us blind and eating us out of house and home, you makes Ned Kelly look like a bloody amateur.'

'You leave Horace alone, Sid Tompkin,' me Mam always shouts at him then. 'Youm only jealous because Horace has made his fortune, and you'll never make yours.'

She still thinks that me Dad is rich, you

know. Even though none of his money has come yet, and none of his luggage neither, she still believes all his excuses about why nothing's come. He told her last week that his lawyers in Australia had sent him word that his Gold Mine needed some new machinery so there was going to be a bit of a delay in sending his money on until the new machinery was installed and the Gold Mine was working again.

Oh yeah, the Gold Mine. I aren't told you about that before, have I. Well, about four weeks ago this letter come addressed to me Dad, and he read it all secretive then threw it on the fire and told me Mam that it was from Australia. I saw the stamps on the envelope when he threw it on the fire. And they was English stamps, so the letter couldn't have come from Australia, could it. But when I told me Mam about the stamps, she just laughed all scoffing and told me, 'That's why youm wearing specs, Specs. Because you can't see proper. You can't see the difference between Australian and English stamps, can you.'

Silly cow!

Anyway, me Dad told her that his lawyers and business advisors had just heard of a wonderful bargain. A Gold

Mine was going for sale really cheap. He said it was right next door to Bondi Beach so it was very convenient for loading the gold onto the ships. He said his lawyers had pressed him to use his Sheep Ranch money to buy the Gold Mine. With a bit of new machinery, and under new management, it would make him one of the richest men in Australia.

'But of course, Effie,' he looked all solemn at her then, 'I should like to have your advice on this matter, before I tell my lawyers to go ahead. Because if I use all my money to buy this gold mine, I shan't have any left to pay you for my bed and board, and I shan't be able to buy that big house just yet neither. So it's up to you, darlint. It's either steak and chips tomorrow, or steak, chips, champagne, yachts, houses, diamonds and furs in a couple of months. What's it to be, darlint?'

She was in heaven!

'Buy the gold mine, Horace, and don't you worry about paying for nothing here. I'll do some more overtime at work,' she told him.

What a daft bat she is! He's telling her he won't have enough money to pay for his bed and board, and the thing is that he arn't paid a penny for his bed and board since he's been back at home here.

And then there's the tale he told her about his luggage.

There was a story in the paper one day about a British ship sinking in the South China Sea.

When me Dad read the story, he said, 'Oh my God! That's the ship all me luggage is on!'

'I knew it!' Sid skreeked. 'I knew that's what you'd say. Didn't I tell everybody that you'd put your bleedin' luggage on the bleedin' *Titanic!* The only thing that surprises me about it is that I didn't think there was any icebergs floating around in the bleedin' South China Sea.'

'That just goes to show how ignorant you am, Sid Tompkin,' me Dad said all sneery and contemptuous. 'Because it's a fact that there are millions of icebergs bigger than this house floating around the South China Sea. They sinks ships there every week.'

Uncle Harold was sat by the table and he said, 'I don't think that information is completely accurate, you know, Horace. I've read extensively, but have yet to discover any accounts of millions of icebergs floating around in the South China Sea.'

Now this is where me Dad boxed really clever. You see he knows that he can't afford to put everybodys back up against him in this house. Me Mam and Virgy are on his side, but me and Sid are against him. Hilda don't count, but Uncle Harold has influence with me Mam, because she thinks the sun shines out of Uncle Harold's backside and if anybody upsets me Uncle Harold she's up in arms against them straight away.

Me Dad just looked Uncle Harold straight in the face, and told him.

'Harold, I bow to your superior knowledge of these matters. if you say that there are no icebergs in the South China Sea, then I accept that statement absolutely and without quibble. In passing may I respectfully bring to your attention the fact that it was Sid Tompkin who said that the ship with my luggage on it had been sunk by an iceberg? I made no such claim as to what sank the vessel.'

Uncle Harold's glasses steamed up, because he was so pleased and charmed with me Dad's answer that he started to cry with joy.

Sid was looking all smug. 'Told you, didn't I, Horace Kensal. You knows nothing! Youm too stupid to see that I was only being sarcastic when I was on about icebergs. I know there's no icebergs there. That ship was more than likely sunk by a submarine.'

'A submarine?' me Dad laughed all scoffingly. 'Has nobody told you yet that the war is over, Sidney Tompkin? Every Jap and German U-boat was sunk years ago. Don't you ever read the papers? Or can't you read?'

Sid still sat looking ever so smug. 'I won't talk about me education, Horace Kensal. I'm not going to be big-yedded and start bragging about me time in Oxford and Cambridge, or the qualifications that I'se got. But I would like to inform you that it could have been a Chink submarine that sank that ship.'

'A bloody Chink?' Me Dad acted like he couldn't believe his ears. 'Why should a bloody Chink sink the ship?'

'Has it escaped your notice, Horace Kensal, that we're fighting the Chinks in Korea?' Sid was triumphant now. 'I rest my case.'

Uncle Harold was looking at the paper

then, and he said, 'Actually, it only states that there has been reports of a ship being sunk. It has yet to be confirmed.'

'Oh Ho! Not confirmed.' Sid was looking very know-all now. 'That's going to put you in a very difficult position, Horace Kensal.'

'What do you mean by that, Sidney Tompkin?' Me Dad was looking wary.

'Well, let us suppose that a report is received that the vessel has not been sunk and is sailing on to England. What excuse will you make for not having any luggage then, that's what I'd like to know? What will you say when the ship comes into harbour, and you still don't get any luggage sent on to here?'

Before me Dad could say anything, Sid rushed to put the wireless on.

'It's time for the news,' he said. 'Let's see what they say about that ship, shall we.'

After a bit of rabbiting the bloke on the wireless said that the reports of a ship being sunk were false, and that the ship in question was in fact sailing on to England.

'Hurrah!' Sid shouted, and he was grinning like a Cheshire Cat. 'Hurrah,

Hurrah Hurrah! I'm off to the pub to celebrate.'

And before anybody could say a word to him, he rushed out of the house.

'That bugger is bloody bonkers. Stark raving mad!' me Dad said.

To tell you the truth, I reckon that Sid and me Dad are both stark raving bonkers. And I'll tell you something else, they're driving me stark raving bonkers as well.

Eleven

Our Virgy has invited Alistair Pickles to Sunday Tea, and he's said yes, and me Mam is really excited about it. She keeps on making lists of what she's going to buy for him to eat, and she says that she's going to have to buy a new tablecloth and cutlery and crockery because our stuff is too old and shabby to put in front of him. And she keeps on bragging to the neighbours about him coming.

Mrs Masters lives at number 33, next door to us, and every time me Mam sees her, she tells her, 'Yes, we're having

Captain Alistair Pickles to tea next Sunday. He's a very important man, you know. He's our Virgy's commanding officer in the Church of Light Army, he is. He's our Virgy's financy as well, only I want to keep that a secret for a bit longer. Because you know how spiteful folks around here can be. They'll only say that our Virgy is marrying Captain Pickles for his money. He comes from a very rich and important family, you know.'

Mrs Masters only smiles and looks at me and winks. I like Mrs Masters, she's always been really nice to me, and she's always laughing and smiling. Not sour-faced and nagging like me Mam.

Another thing me Mam is doing is trying to make up her mind about who she's going to let have tea with Alistair Pickles. She says that me Dad will have to be there, because he's Virgy's proper Dad, but Sid will have to go out somewhere, because he aren't Virgy's proper Dad, and she doesn't want Alistair Pickles to know anything about Sid living in our house. She says that Alistair Pickles might get the wrong idea.

Sid gets all mad when she says that.

'Wrong idea? Wrong idea? How can you say that, Effie, when me and you has been living over the brush for so many years? And I brought your kids up like they was me own. I've been more of a proper Dad to Virgy than Horace Kensal ever was.'

'Hold on a minute, Sid Tompkin,' me Dad pipes up then. 'Let me tell you that I was slaving in the Outback to make my fortune for the sake of my missus and kids. I've suffered years of heartbreak and hardship just so that one day I could come and cover my missus and kids in diamonds. That's what I'se done. That's what being a Dad is all about.'

Sid gets all sarcastic then. 'Certainly you have been slaving for years, Horace Kensal,' he says all silky and smooth. 'And just look at all the diamonds covering your missus and kids right this minute. They dazzle my eyes!'

'That's enough from both of you.' Me Mam cracks the whip, and they both shut up.

I can't take it in, you know, how scared they both am of me Mam. She's the boss in this house, alright.

Uncle Harold can come to tea, me Mam decides, because he's very genteel and it will show Captain Pickles that our family is as posh as anybody. But Hilda will have to go out somewhere, because she's living in sin and she's a Scarlet Woman, and Captain Pickles is a man of God who'd be mortally offended if he had to sit and eat his tea in company with such a sinner.

Poor old Hilda! She starts to cry when me Mam says this, and me Mam tells her, 'Now stop bloody blarting, Hilda. You can come back in again when Captain Pickles has gone.'

'What about me, Mam?' I ask her.

I don't really want to have tea with them, but she reckons she's going to buy salmon and ham and all sorts of other nice things to eat, and I shouldn't mind having some of them.

Me Mam shakes her head. 'After giving the matter some thought, Specs, I think it'll be for the best if you go out somewhere as well. You're a bit too scruffy, and you aren't got anything nice to wear. That blue suit of yours looks like summat you got off the Rag and Bone man.'

Well, I like that! I don't think! Who was it who stopped me getting a brand-new gaberdine full drape with a single button, and new brothel-creepers and a silk tie with a picture on it, and a long pointed-collared shirt, I should like to know? Who was it who spent all the money I'd saved to buy meself a new gaberdine suit with? And now she calls me scruffy.

Uncle Harold pipes up then. 'Effie, my dear, I do think that in the circumstances it might be best if Specs was allowed to have tea with us. I'm positive that a Christian officer and gentleman like Captain Pickles would enjoy and appreciate meeting a family such as ours who are united in love and harmony.'

Blimey! United in Love and Harmony? Our family? Do you know, there's times I wonder if Uncle Harold is living in the same world as I am. I mean, I know that he lives in this house with me, but is he really here? I reckon his body is, but the rest of him is off wandering around somewhere else most of the time.

'But what's he going to wear, Our Harold?' me Mam wanted to know. 'He can't sit down to tea wearing that bloody old blue suit of his, can he. It 'ud put Captain Pickles straight off his food to see the state of that suit.'

Harold nodded all wisely. 'I might have the solution to that problem, Effle, my dear. You may leave it in my hands.'

'Hold on a minute,' I tell them both.

'I don't know if I want to come to tea anyway.'

Me Mam went mad then and started ranting and raving at me.

'You'll do what you're told, you ungrateful young bugger. As long as youm living in my house you'll do what I tell you to do. I'm in charge of you until yourn eighteen, and don't you forget it. I can have you put away into a home if you don't do what I tell you to.'

I'm sure that she's mental sometimes, you know. She scares everybody else in the house when she goes off her trolley like this. To tell you the truth, she scares me a bit as well.

So, it looks like I'll be having me tea with them, after all. But I don't know what I'll be wearing ...

Twelve

I reckon that today has been the worst day of my life. I like Saturdays, you know, and I look forwards to Saturday all the rest of the week. But this Saturday has been horrible!

On Saturday we only work 'til twelve o'clock on the Gas, and then we're finished 'til Monday morning. But before I went to work this morning me Mam told me, 'Come back here as soon as you finish work, Specs. There's something very important I wants you to do this afternoon.'

Well, that makes me feel miserable straight away. Because I like to have a wander about on Saturday afternoons, and go and see if I can find any adventures.

When I got to work Georgie Snood was in a rotten temper because of the beer he drunk last night. He's always in a bad temper first thing on Saturday and Monday mornings, then after a couple of hours he cheers up a bit. But this morning he never cheered up at all.

We was supposed to put a new gas pipe into this house, you see, and the pipe had got to run along a trench. Well, he made me dig the trench, and the ground wasn't half hard. All rocky. And he just sat on his backside watching me and shouting at me all the time.

'Get a move on, you lazy sod!'

'Get your finger out, 'ull you.'

'Youm bloody useless, you am. You'll

never make a Gas Fitter as long as you'se got a'nole in your arse.'

He threw the hammer at me first, but he missed. Then a bit later on he threw the stilsons at me, but I was lucky because just as he threw them I bent down to pull a rock out and they went over me head. But the next thing he threw at me was the blowlamp, and that hit me on the back of me head, and it didn't half hurt.

Now I know that I hit him back before, but to tell you the truth I'm scared of doing it again, because I know that the next time I do hit him back he'll go to the police for sure, and make them put me into prison. He's told me so about a hundred times. And he says that it's his duty to teach me how to be a proper Gas Fitter, and that the proper way to teach me is to give me a clout when I makes mistakes, because that's the only way I'll ever remember not to make the same mistake again.

When the blowlamp hit me I shouted, 'Hey, just pack it in. That hurt, that did.'

'O'course it hurt,' he told me. 'It was meant to hurt. Gas Fitters' Mates has been getting hurt for making balls-ups ever since the first gasworks was ever built in the days of the Pharoahs.'

'There wasn't any gasworks in the days of the Pharoahs,' I told him.

'That just shows how little you knows about the Gas, Specs,' he come back at me. 'What the bloody hell does you think them pyramids are?'

'Tombs,' I said.

'They'm bloody gasometers, you stupid daft berk,' he shouted, and I just give up then. What's the use of arguing against an idiot?

I was really glad when twelve o'clock came, I'll tell you.

When I got home me Mam was waiting for me with Uncle Harold and he was all dressed up in his black funeral clothes. He had his top hat on, and tailcoat and a long cloak, and round his hat he'd wrapped masses of black ribbons and they was dangling down to his shoulders. He was looking all excited, and his glasses kept on steaming up so me Mam had to keep on wiping them clear for him.

'You've got to go and help your Uncle Harold this afternoon, Specs,' me Mam told me. 'And I don't want any argument about it neither.'

‘Help him to do what?’ I asked.

Uncle Harold was shaking all over he was so excited.

‘Today is ‘D Day’, Specs. You and I are going to make history today. This day will be embossed in letters of gold in the annals of this glorious industry. After today our fame will resound all over the Undertaking World.’

‘What are we going to do then, Uncle Harold?’ I can’t take this in, you know. Why he’s all excited like this, I mean.

‘We are going to unveil to an eager world my “Sweet Dreams Mobile Resting Haven”. And you, Specs, are going to share the glory with me.’

Blimey! I don’t want to have anything to do with it.

Me Mam is looking very fierce at me though. ‘Smiling Sam has sent you these clothes you’ve got to wear, Specs. And he’s very kindly agreed to let you keep them to wear tomorrow when Captain Pickles comes round for his tea.’

I told her that I wasn’t going to do it, but then she went mental at me, and I had to give in. The clothes were horrible. An old black suit and a top hat just like me Uncle Harold’s, but the top hat was too big for me head so me Mam stuffed it with newspaper until it ledged on top of me head. When I looked at meself in the glass I felt like crying.

Then Hilda come downstairs wearing a long black dress and covered all over in black veils.

'I thought you said that Hilda hadn't got to do this again, Mam?' I can't take it in, I really can't.

'Everybody has got to help Harold to make this a big success,' me Mam said all snotty. 'And besides, she's doing the "Dark Angel" today, not the "Spirit of Death, so it's more tasteful and not morbid.'

Uncle Harold was grinning all over his face. 'It's going to be a "Biggie", Specs. A real "Biggie". We're going to be a sensation!'

Tommy TeeTee and Bertie Shellshock come round the back door then. Tommy was in his Salvation Army uniform and wellies, and Bertie Shellshock was wearing a bowler hat and an old army greatcoat dyed black.

'Behold, my Charioteers.' Uncle Harold was the happiest I've ever seen him.

I got a bit worried then.

'I can't pull the "Sweet Dreams Mobile

Resting Haven" on my own, Uncle Harold. It's too big,' I told him.

'You haven't got to pull it, Specs. I'm hiring Old Charlie's horse to do that. All you'll have to do is to lead the horse along. It'll be ever so easy for you to do.'

I don't care how easy it is, I don't want to do it. I don't want anybody to see me dressed up in these clothes and with a top hat on me head.

''Ull you stop pulling your bleedin' face about, Specs,' me Mam skreeked. 'Try to look cheerful, 'ull you.'

Cheerful? I thought it was a funeral we're going to, not a party.

'Whose funeral is it anyway?' I asked me Uncle Harold.

'It's Shylock Dolton's missus,' Uncle Harold told me. 'He's getting it for nothing because it's the trial run.'

Shylock Dolton, the 'Meanest Man in England'! He wouldn't give a blind man the time, not even if he was wearing two watches. He'd sell it to him.

'Of course Shylock took a bit of persuading to let us have his missus for our trial run,' Uncle Harold said. 'At first he said that we couldn't have her because he was having her cremated so he could put her ashes on his potato bed because he reckons ashes are good for the soil. He said that his missus might as well make herself useful, now that she'd put him to all the trouble of arranging her funeral.'

Uncle Harold looked all preened up and proud of himself then. 'Do you know, Specs, though I say it myself, I regard my diplomacy on this occasion as one of my finest achievements since I joined the Undertaking industry. First of all I persuaded Smiling Sam to pay Shylock a fee for letting us have Mrs Shylock to practise with. And then I went to see Quasimodo, and persuaded him to let me have the use of one of his prepared graves at the discount price.'

Quasimodo is the grave digger down at the cemetery. Him and Uncle Harold used to be bitter enemies, but they're friends now. Uncle Harold says that their friendship has grown because of their mutual respect for each other's expertise in their chosen vocations.

He does come out with some weird stuff, me Uncle Harold, don't he.

'What do you mean?' I can't take this in, you know.

'It's quite simple, Specs. Quasimodo

always has a couple of graves ready dug waiting for customers. He's agreed to let us practise tipping Old Shylock's missus into one of them. And then, once we're satisfied that our technique has been perfected, we can leave her in it, because he's dug it a bit deeper to make the extra room. That's why we're getting the discount because he can still use the hole for someone else.'

Uncle Harold was smiling all dreamily.

'I pointed out to Shylock that he'd make a sizeable profit, and he'd even save money on shoe leather because he didn't have to come down to the cemetery. And he finally agreed to let us have her. So all is for the best, in the best of all possible worlds, Specs. We can have as many trial runs as we want.'

It still don't sound right to me. What about the service? Who's going to conduct that? When I ask me Uncle Harold, he just shrugs it off.

'Shylock says he's making the arrangements for that.'

He goes to the back door and tells Tommy TeeTee and Bertie Shellshock, 'Now, Gentlemen, make ready! Destiny awaits us. Let us be gone from here. Come on, Hilda, Specs.'

I don't half feel a right prat walking down the street with this lot. There's Uncle Harold with his cloak blowing in the wind, waving his black flag and strutting along in front, and Hilda and Tommy TeeTee and Bertie Shellshock marching along behind him swinging their arms like soldiers, and there's me bringing up the rear, with me top hat under me arm, trying to look as if I'm not with them.

All the neighbours come to watch us go past, and Mrs Masters shouted, 'It's the Prussian Guard.'

Everybody starts laughing, and a bloke tells us, 'You've left it a bit late to march into Russia. Old Adolf went off without you.'

It goes on like that all the way down to the cemetery, only most of what they shouted at us is too rude to tell you.

Filthy Cyril, Old Charlie's son, is waiting with the horse down at the Old Chapel in the cemetery. He really is a City Slicker alright. Dirty ragged old overcoat and trilby hat. A beard and long hair hanging to his shoulders. No shirt or vest, just a waistcoat, his trousers all torn and his boots holey. He's got no socks on, but it don't matter much because his feet are so black you'd think he was wearing socks. And he don't half smell. The horse looks and smells about the same.

The trouble starts now. The horse won't let me come near it, or anybody else except Filthy Cyril, so in the end Uncle Harold has to give Filthy Cyril ten bob to join the procession because he's the only one that can lead the horse. Mind you, there's no problem with what he's wearing because it's all so black and filthy it fits in with the colour of the rest of our uniforms.

Then Hilda starts to play up.

Uncle Harold wants her to sit on top of the 'Sweet Dreams Mobile Resting Haven' and pretend that she's the Dark Angel. Only Hilda's scared of heights, so she starts blarting and hanging onto the wheel of the 'Haven' while Uncle Harold and Tommy TeeTee and Bertie Shellshock are all trying to push her up on top of it. Hilda's only small and skinny, but she's ever so strong, and they can't budge her.

Uncle Harold is so disappointed that he starts to cry, and his glasses steam up, so he can't see anything.

Hilda's sorry then. So she tells him, 'If I get up there, Harold, dearest, will you promise to marry me as soon as we can get the banns called?'

So after a bit of argument Uncle Harold promises, and she lets them push her up on top. But she's still scared of heights, so what she does is to lie on her front all along the top and hang on to the sides.

After he wiped his glasses Uncle Harold stared up at her for a long time, and then he told me, 'Do you know, Specs, I find Hilda's pose very effective. It appears that the Dark Angel is caressing the Dear Newly Departed and welcoming her onto the "Other Side". I find the tableau pleases me greatly, Specs. It is both artistically and emotionally moving.' He gave me a tin drum then. 'Will you carry this for me, please, Specs. I'll tell you what it's for later.'

We had to go up the hill to get through the town to Shylock Dolton's house. Uncle Harold was marching in front, and after him come Filthy Cyril leading the horse and Haven with Hilda laying down on top of it. Then Tommy TeeTee and Bertie Shellshock pushing the prams with the bags of dirt in them, and two plaster cherubs each. Uncle Harold said he wanted to create a big splash so he was going to use every available cherub he had. I said

I had to tie me shoelaces up, and hung right back behind, with me hat under one arm, and me drum under the other. I felt a right prat, especially when they went past the pub at the bottom of the hill and all the blokes come running out to cheer and clap them. Georgie Snood was one of these blokes, and when he saw me he went mental.

'Look who it aren't,' he kept shouting and roaring with laughing. 'It's the Black Death himself. Specs the Dark Destroyer!'

Very funny, I don't think.

Halfway up the hill the horse lay down, and wouldn't shift. Uncle Harold had to give all the blokes from the pub two bob each to help us pull and push the horse and Haven up to the top of the hill. As soon as we got there, the horse got up again. He's always been dead crafty that Co-op horse has, you know. Poor Uncle Harold was nearly crying by then, because he's spent all his money and had to borrow me last five bob from me even, to finish paying off the blokes who was pushing and pulling.

Well, we managed to get to Shylock Dolton's house and he was waiting for us with his face as miserable as sin. That's not really his name, Shylock, it's what everybody calls him for being so mean. He's tighter than a duck's backside, you know.

'Youm late,' he shouted at Uncle Harold. 'Don't you know that time is money?'

'Well, you aren't paying for anything, are you,' I told him sharpish. I was feeling really fed up, you know, and I'm not scared of Shylock Dolton.

'Well, let's get on with it,' he said. 'I've wasted enough of the bloody day already.'

'Where is the Dear Departed?' Uncle Harold asked him.

'The same place that she's been for the last week.' Shylock was looking daggers at all of us. 'Where else do you think she'd be? She aren't likely to go off running around the town, is she, the condition she's in.'

Of course Shylock and his missus hated each other, you know. She was a horrible tight old cow, as well. Worse than him even. When their kids started work, Missus Shylock used to take all their wages off them because she said they owed her thousands for their keep since they'd been born, and they had their kids working just as soon as they could walk about a bit.

Their eldest kid, Barry, told me once that he was doing a paper round when he was three years old. He said that he was so small he had to drag the bag behind him on the ground, and he got the sack because he was wearing out the bags too quick. The kids soon run off to Australia and Canada and New Zealand, I can tell you, and never ever wrote to Shylock and his missus again.

Shylock's kids used to be called the 'Bisto Kids', because to save money Shylock only fed them a little bit of food, and they used to go round the town's fish and chip shops all day and stand outside the doors sniffing the smells of the chips and fish, and people used to feel sorry for them when they saw them so skinny and sometimes they'd give them money to buy food with, but the Doltons owns four rows of houses in the town, and they charges real high rents, so Shylock has always had plenty of money.

I wish I had plenty of money. I'd marry Sophia or Glenda Shortway and buy a big house to live in, and a car, and a television, and I'd stop working at the Gas, and do a job that I liked doing. I might still join the Foreign Legion. They'd make me an officer if I was rich, wouldn't they. I should really like that. And Sophia or Glenda could live in a tent in the desert and I could ride up to see her every night, just like Ronald Colman used to ride up and see his girlfriend in that film, *Under Two Flags*. I'd probably grow a moustache like Ronald Colman's as well.

Anyway, when we got to Shylock's house Uncle Harold asked him, 'Where's the vicar?'

'Vicar? What does I need the vicar for?' Shylock didn't half pull his face about.

'To conduct the burial service,' Uncle Harold told him.

'I can do that meself. I don't need to waste money on a vicar.'

Uncle Harold looked a bit shocked when Shylock told him that.

Mrs Shylock was in her coffin in the shed down the bottom of the back garden. We was going to take the Haven down the entry, but the horse wouldn't go down it, so Uncle Harold said we'd have to carry the coffin between us, and have the burial service outside Shylock's front door.

All of the neighbours was coming out to watch what was happening, and people were running up from the other streets as well.

We didn't half have a job to bring Mrs Shylock from the shed. Hilda wouldn't come down from the top of the Haven to help us. Me Uncle Harold said he had to stay with the Haven and get it ready to receive the Dear Departed. Filthy Cyril just looked blank when we asked him to help and Shylock said he wasn't one of the hired help and he wasn't supposed to carry her, so in the end it was just me, Tommy TeeTee and Bertie Shellshock. It took us ages, because the coffin wasn't half heavy so we had to drag it along and keep stopping to rest and get our breaths back.

'How come she's got so bleedin' heavy?' Tommy TeeTee kept moaning.

To tell you the truth, I was wondering about that, as well. Because the last time I saw her she looked so skinny that a puff of wind would have blown her over.

When we got the coffin to the side of the Haven we couldn't lift it up to slide it inside, not until some of the neighbours come and helped us.

'Gawd strewth, Shylock!' one of the blokes puffed out. 'Has you wrapped her in lead, or summat? I reckon I've ruptured meself lifting her up.'

'Just mind your own business,' Shylock told him. 'And let me get on with the service.' Then he banged on the side of the coffin and shouted, 'Ashes to ashes, dust to dust, if God won't take you, then the Devil must. Off you jolly well go, Flower.'

All the neighbours started booing and hissing him, but he didn't give a monkey's for that, and just went back into his house and slammed the door shut.

Bertie Shellshock and Tommy TeeTee brought their chariots alongside, and we had to put all the bags of dirt on top of the coffin, which was a bit hard to do, because Hilda wouldn't move off the top so we had to pile the bags in from the side entrance, and it made it ever so hard for us. Then Uncle Harold got all depressed because we couldn't put the cherubs where he wanted them on top of the Haven, because with Hilda laying along the top there wasn't any room for them.

'This is not what I envisaged, Specs,' he kept on telling me. 'This is totally at variance with my scenario for this debut ceremony.'

I was feeling so fed up that all I wanted to do was to run off. But every time I thought of clearing off, I kept on remembering me Mam's face when she goes mental at me, and I lost me nerve and stayed.

It took ages to get to the cemetery, because every few yards the horse kept on laying down, and we had to keep asking people to come and help us lift it up again. All me suit was muddy from the mud on the horse, and everybody was laughing at us. And when we went through the town who should come walking down the road but Glenda Shortway with all her mates. They all started screaming with laughing and taking the mickey. One of them kept on shouting, 'Look, Glenda, it's that kid who's sweet on you. He looks like Dracula's uncle, don't he. Don't you let him ever take you for a ride in his coffin. He's a vampire, he is.'

I was nearly crying, you know.

Glenda Shortway will never marry me now, will she.

When we got to the hill we had to go down towards the cemetery. We didn't half have a job to keep the Haven from getting away from us, it was so heavy. All the blokes come out of the pub again and we had to lash long ropes around the Haven and all pull on them to hold it back. I couldn't take it in, you know. Why was Mrs Shylock so heavy?

There was a massive crowd following us now, right down into the cemetery they came, and the police came as well to keep the crowd in order, and the photographer from the paper came, and the reporter as well.

Funny enough, Uncle Harold was crowing with joy. His eyes was shining and he kept on telling me, 'Wonderful, Specs! This is wonderful. I'm going to be famous. My Haven is going to be famous. This is wonderful, Specs. I told you that we'd be a sensation, did I not.'

Quasimodo was waiting at the graveside all dressed up in his best suit and with his ceremonial spade. It's all burnished and glittering, that spade is. He don't use it to dig with, only to stand and pose with when it's an important funeral.

Mrs Shylock's funeral aren't important, not like the Chairman of the Council's or anybody like that, but because it's Uncle Harold's big day, and they're such good mates now, Quasimodo is doing his bit by parading in his ceremonial outfit.

Quasimodo is the spitting image of the Hunchback of Notre Dame in the film, you know. He's got a big lump on his back, one shoulder is higher than the other, and his eyes are all skew-whiffted. And he spends hours swinging on the branches of the trees down in the cemetery, just like the Hunchback swings from the bells.

By the time we got the Haven lined up with the grave we was all sweating and gasping, but we had a rest then because we had to wait for Smiling Sam to come.

The crowds was getting a bit restless while we waited, and they kept on shouting, 'Cummon, gerron with it!'

And singing, 'Why are we waiting? Whyee are weee waiting? Whyeee are weeee waiting?'

And Tommy TeeTee started shouting back at them, 'This is an illegal assembly. Disperse in the Queen's name. Disperse or we fire!'

And him and Bertie Shellshock started chucking stones at the crowd, and they was shouting and chucking stones back at him and Bertie Shellshock until the police stopped the battle.

Then Smiling Sam came and brought KKKKKatie Coffin, his missus, with him. Everybody calls her that because she stutters. And he brought some of his mates who are on the Council as well. All bigwigs in the town. Everybody was trying to get into the act now, and Uncle Harold was crying with joy.

'I'm a success, Specs,' he kept telling me, while I was wiping his glasses for him. 'I'm a success at last.'

Smiling Sam was rubbing his hands, and chuckling. 'We're going to be rich, Harold. We're going to be bloody millionaires. What a happy day this is.'

'It aren't a happy day for Mrs Shylock, is it,' KKKKKatie Coffin told him, all sour.

She's always miserable, she is, you know. She likes spoiling everybody's enjoyment.

Uncle Harold took the drum off me then and give it to Bertie Shellshock. Bertie started hammering the drum and me Uncle Harold did his trumpet imitation and blew the 'Last Post'.

Some of the women started crying because they said it was so very moving.

Uncle Harold was almost bursting with pride when he stepped up to the lever and pulled it to send Mrs Shylock down into the grave.

The coffin shot out like a bullet, and hit the bottom of the hole so hard that it burst open, and a big pile of rocks and rubbish fell out of it. There was no sign of Mrs Shylock at all.

KKKKKatie Coffin fainted, and Tommy TeeTee was so shocked he fell down into the hole on top of the coffin. At least he said afterwards that it was the shock, but I reckon it was because he was drunk. You see the trouble is with Tommy TeeTee you can never tell the difference between when he's drunk and when he's sober. He's as daft as a brush all the time.

Uncle Harold just stood there with his eyes bulging, but Smiling Sam went mental.

'He's done you, you daft bugger!' he skreeked at Uncle Harold. 'Bloody Shylock Dolton's done you!'

The crowd was all cheering and clapping and laughing, and then the horse bolted, and the Haven went bouncing over the gravestones and Hilda was hanging on top of it skreeking, 'Save me, Harold!! Save me, Harold! Save me! Save me!'

'You're sacked!' Smiling Sam shouted at Harold, and went storming off.

Then a bloke come up and told us, 'I've only just found out what's been going on here. I'm from the Crematorium, and Shylock Dolton had his missus cremated there three days ago. If you go down to his allotment you'll see her scattered across his potato patch, she's the white bits.'

Uncle Harold had another of his nervous breakdowns then. So I had to lead him back home and put him to bed.

Of course me Mam was pestering to know what had happened, so after a bit I told her.

'Why didn't you make sure who was in the bloody coffin?' she skreeked at me.

I couldn't believe it, when she said that.

'It wasn't nothing to do with me who was in the coffin,' I told her. 'It wasn't my job to find out. And anyway, why should we think that Shylock Dolton was doing us?'

'Because Shylock Dolton does everybody, you daft bugger! Do you know summat, Specs, you've even lost the half a brain cell you was born with.'

I just cleared off then, because I was feeling really fed up with it all, and went to call for Johnny Merry to see if he was coming to the dance at the Memorial Hall.

But he wasn't there, so I had to spend the rest of the night mooching about on me own. It wasn't half depressing, I can tell you.

Thirteen

Captain Pickles didn't come to tea today. He sent ever such a snotty note to me Mam. It said:

'To whom it may concern,
Captain Alistair Pickles wishes to make it known that he no longer wishes to associate with Miss Virginia Kensal, or any other member, relation or friend of the Kensal family.
Signed Captain Alistair Pickles,
Church of Light Army.'

Of course me Mam blamed me for him not coming.

'What else does you expect, after the show up you made of yourself yesterday at that bloody funeral!' she kept on skreeking at me. 'An important man like Captain Pickles aren't going to want to ate his tea with a bloody No Good like you.'

Well, I like that, I don't think! What did I do? Nothing? It wasn't my fault what happened, was it. And who was it made me go to the funeral, I'd like to know? Who was it went mental at me when I said I wouldn't go to the funeral? Who was it made me wear that rotten top hat and suit?

'I knew it 'ud all end in tears, Effie,' Snidey Sid had to put his oar in then, didn't he. 'I told you what 'ud happen, didn't I.'

'And you can bloody well shurrup, as well!' Me Mam went for him like a tiger.

Me Dad thought he could see an opportunity to get one up on Sid.

'Now, now, Effie, darlint,' he said all smarmy. 'Try not to upset yourself, darlint. Remember I'm here to comfort you. I'm the rock that you can stand on.'

'Youm the bloody rock round me neck dragging me down into ruin,' she skreeked at him.

And he swallowed all hard and shut up.

Uncle Harold was upstairs laying in bed, and Hilda was sitting by him stroking his forehead with a damp flannel.

When I went up to see how he was Hilda skreeked at me, 'This is all your fault, Specs! I begged my poor Harold not to have anything to do with you. And now look at the poor lamb. He's laying here next to death's door. And it's all your fault!'

All my fault? I can't take this in, you know.

'Will you tell her, Uncle Harold?' I begged him.

But he only looked at me, all pale and forlorn and whispered, 'I want you to know that I forgive you, Specs. And if I die tonight, I want to have these words inscribed on my tomb: "I, Harold Augustus Smith, wish to make it known that I forgive my nephew, Specs Kensal, for the dreadful wrong he has done me".'

I put me head round the door of the front bedroom to see how our Virgy was, and she was laying on the bed all tearful and forlorn.

'How are you feeling, Virgy?' I asked all sympathetic.

'Go away, you Demon!' she skreeked. 'You've ruined my life! I'll never ever be happy again. I wish I was dead. Go away, you evil spawn of Satan!'

Blimey! That's her and Doreen Merry who thinks the Devil is me Dad. Come to think of it, he probably is.

I went back downstairs and me Mam was in the scullery, and Sid and me Dad both glared at me, and started hissing:

'Are you happy now, you cruel swine?'

'Are you satisfied with what you've done?'

'You've destroyed this family, you unnatural young devil!'

'I can't believe that youm a son of mine!'

I give up then, and went out.

I'll tell you something, shall I. As soon as I get enough money for me passport and ticket, I'm going straight to France to join the Foreign Legion.

Fourteen

The Fair's here this week. So every night me and Johnny Merry and the rest of our gang go down to the Rec where the Fair sets up. That's the Old Recreation Ground down the town. The Fair comes twice a year, and it comes to places round about another few times, so we goes to those other places as well. But it's best when it comes to our own town, because in the other places the local gangs don't like us coming there, and sometimes we have to fight with them. I don't mind having to fight them, but the trouble is I have to take me glasses off when I get into a fight and then I can't see very well, so I get hit more than I should if I could see better.

When I was a kid we used to have fights against the gangs from the other streets in our town, and I always used to think that when we left school and started work we wouldn't have fights with other gangs, but we still do. Only now, instead of fighting with gangs from the other streets in our own town, we fight with gangs from the streets in other towns. It's weird, aren't it.

My friend Mr Sambourn told me that all young blokes have to pass through their 'Rites of Passage'. Yeah, that's what he said. 'Rites of Passage.'

He says that it's all a necessary part of gaining experience of life, and that we're only following nature's intended course, and that if we was living in the old days we would have to undergo certain trials of endurance and tests of courage before we would be accepted as men and warriors.

He says that's the reason that we form our gangs and fight each other. We're following our natural instincts.

Mr Sambourn is the cleverest bloke I've ever met, you know. You ought to see inside his house, it's all books wherever you look. There must be thousands of them. He keeps on telling me, 'Read, Specs. Read voraciously and indiscriminately. Read for pleasure, for profit and for knowledge. But do not withdraw from life. Go out into the world and embrace every experience that you are able to.'

He says he'll teach me how to play chess if I want. When I told him that I was too thick to learn a difficult game like that he told me, 'Specs, you are making the common mistake of equating education with intelligence. You may be uneducated, Specs, but you are certainly not unintelligent. Some of the most highly educated people I know are in certain aspects the most stupid also.'

When I told him that I'm going to join the Foreign Legion and have adventures, he didn't laugh at me like the others do. He just smiled.

'You do that, Specs. Life in the Legion can be very hard and brutal, but life is not meant to be all soft beds and gentleness.'

Me Mam hates me being friends with Mr Sambourn though. She says it aren't natural for a kid like me to be friends with an old bloke like him. She says that old blokes like him who are nice to young kids are all arsehole bandits. That's a rotten thing to say, aren't it. I know a couple of old blokes in the town who are arsehole bandits chasing after the kids, but Mr Sambourn aren't like that. He's just a smashing old bloke.

Me Mam says that he's a snob, as well, and that he thinks he's better than working class people because he talks posh and he don't talk about football and horse racing and pigeons and play dominos and crib like blokes do. But he's not a snob at all. He's just interested in other sorts of things instead of football and horse racing and pigeons and dominos and crib.

Anyway, I don't care what she says, I shall still stay friends with Mr Sambourn.

I told you that me and the gang went to the fair last night, didn't I. It was great. Johnny Merry and me had a go in the Boxing Booth, and Mad Jack did a demonstration dive from off the Swing

Boats. Yeah, he did, really. He dived off the Swing Boats.

We'd only just got to the Fairground and we was mooching about seeing who was there and suddenly there was a big commotion by the Swing Boats. Everybody was running towards them, and there was a lot of shouting and screaming going on. So we run with the rest.

When we got to the Swing Boats we could see this one boat with two blokes in it going really high so that it was nearly going right over the top bar and almost upside down.

'It's Mad Jack and Filthy Cyril,' a kid I know told me. 'They'm trying to "Loop the Loop."'

I've told you about Filthy Cyril, haven't I. Well, his best mate is 'Mad Jack'. He's Filthy Cyril's only mate really, that's if you don't count all the fleas and bugs he carries about with him.

Mad Jack looks like Filthy Cyril, as well, a real City Slicker!

People say that when Mad Jack was a kid he was a brilliant diver, and he was really clever as well, until one day he went to the Swimming Baths and he dived off the top board, but somehow or other he managed to hit his head on the bottom of the pool and when he come out of the water he was Doolally Tap, and he's stayed Doolally Tap ever since. He still does a lot of diving though, down at the Coal Yard. The Coalmen gives him a few bob to dive off the top of the wall into the piles of coal sacks. But he's not allowed into the Swimming Baths anymore because he turns the water black with coal dust.

He used to sleep rough anywhere he could crawl into at nights, but then him and Filthy Cyril became best mates and he moved into the Rag and Bone Yard as a lodger. He really fits in there very well, you know. Some people reckon that he's Charlie and Daisy's son because he looks like them and dresses and stinks just like the rest of the family. But I don't see how people can say that because Charlie and Daisy and Filthy Cyril and Mad Jack are all so dirty and black that you can't tell what they really look like under the layers.

Anyway, like I was saying, Mad Jack and Filthy Cyril were trying to Loop the Loop. To make the Swing Boat go right over the top bar in a big circle.

All the blokes tries to Loop the Loop,

but I've never seen anybody manage it. People say that years ago somebody did it, but to tell you the truth I reckon it's a load of bullshit. Because if the Swing Boat goes in a big circle over the top bar then it'll turn upside down, won't it. And that means whoever is sitting in it will fall out, won't they. They can't stop from falling out because nobody's strapped in, are they. There's no belts or anything to get strapped in with, is there.

But nobody seems to care about there being no belts or anything, and lots of the young blokes tries to Loop the Loop every time the Fair comes here. The Fair bloke who runs the Swing Boats goes mad when he sees anybody trying, and he bawls and cusses and runs to shove the brake plank up so that it catches on the bottom of the Swing Boat and starts to bring it to a stop.

When we got to the Swing Boats Mad Jack and Filthy Cyril was going really high, and the crowd was cheering and shouting, 'Gooo Onnn! Gooo onnnn! Gooo onnn!''

And the Fair bloke was going mad and rushing to lift the brake plank up, only when he did the Swing Boat hit down on it and the hinge broke and the brake plank fell down again and wouldn't work.

'Hurrah! Hurrah!' the crowd was bawling. 'Gooo onnn! Gooo onnn! Gooo onnn!'

And the Swing Boat went higher and higher, and Mad Jack and Filthy Cyril was stood up in the Boat heaving on the ropes like mad things.

Then the Fair bloke went charging off shouting, 'Police! Police! Help, Police!'

And in a couple of minutes a lot of coppers come running back with him, and they was all shouting to Mad Jack and Filthy Cyril to come down off the Boat. But they didn't take any notice, only kept on heaving and laughing like Boris Karloff does in the pictures when he's playing an evil maniac. Then, the next thing we knew was that Mad Jack come flying out of the Boat and high up over the crowd like he was a bird, flapping his arms like wings and still laughing, and he come tumbling down and landed right on top of two of the coppers.

They had to send for the ambulance then, and take all three to the hospital.

When they got to the hospital the doctors examined them and Mad Jack hadn't got a scratch on him! But the two coppers had all sorts of broken bones, and the doctors reckoned that the coppers would have to stay in hospital for months, but Mad Jack could leave right away.

But when he come walking out of the hospital the other coppers arrested him and he's been charged with 'Grievous Bodily Harm', and also with 'Dangerous Flying'. They arrested Filthy Cyril as well, and charged him with 'Drunken Driving of a Swing Boat'.

They're both out on bail.

Johnny Merry reckons that the bail was a cartload of scrap iron and two dozen rabbitskins from the Rag and Bone Yard.

I'll tell you about the Boxing Booth now, shall I. What happens is that the booth boxers all lines up on the platform in front of the big tent and the bloke in charge of them challenges anybody in the crowd to stay in the ring for three rounds with any of his boxers. If you can last three rounds you get five pounds, but if you can beat the booth boxer you get ten pounds. That's a lot of money, so there's always some blokes ready to have a go.

Well, we was standing in front of the booth and the booth boss was shouting, 'Come on then, is there anybody here brave enough to take on my boys? Or are you all fritted? Three rounds is all you has to last for to win five pounds. It's money for jam. Especially if you're a fast runner and my lads can't catch you. Come on, who's man enough to have a go? Let's see what you're made of. Let's see the best man in the town step up here and prove that he's a fighting man. If any of you can beat any of my boys, then I'll pay you ten pounds in your hand. Ten pounds. You'll be rich! Ten pounds!'

We was all broke, but none of us fancied getting into the ring with the booth boxers because they're really tough, so we didn't say anything. And then the boss pointed at us, and said, 'You look like you're desperate characters. Why don't some o' you have a try?'

'I don't think so,' Johnny Merry told him. 'We're lovers, not fighters.'

'Lovers?' The boss was all sneery, 'What girl in her right senses 'ud want to have wankers like you for lovers? But wait a minute, I can see my mistake now. You lot have come from the Girl's School, haven't you? You're girls, not blokes.'

Then he shouted to the crowd, 'Why

should England tremble, my Lords, Ladies and Gentlemen, with articles like these to defend her? Will you just look how scared they are.'

Then he bowed to us and told us, 'I'm very sorry for frightening you, Girls.'

Johnny Merry got mad then, because he's not scared of anything. 'Who're you calling a girl, you old fart!' he shouted at the boss, and the boss told him, 'You lot, I'm calling you lot girls.'

Some of the blokes in the crowd started laughing, and Johnny Merry told me, 'Come on, Specs. We'll show that old fart whether we'em scared or not.'

He went and jumped up on the platform and like an idiot, I went with him.

'Bring on your best men and me and my mate 'ull take them on,' Johnny shouted.

All the crowd started cheering and clapping, and the boss looked ever so pleased, and shouted, 'We accept the challenge of these brave fighting men. Roll up and pay at the box, my Lords, Ladies and Gentlemen, the programme starts in five minutes.'

Johnny told him, 'You'll have to let the rest of our mates in for nothing, because we're all broke.'

The boss waved 'um over and they all went in for nothing. Then he sent one of the boxers round the back of the tent with me and Johnny Merry to fix us up with some boxing gloves.

'Who shall we be fighting?' I wanted to know, and the boxer just grinned.

'You're in luck today, lads. You're going to be fighting the two evillest, nastiest, roughest, toughest blokes we got, Killer Diller and Mauler Malloy. I wouldn't get in the ring with either of 'um for a pension meself. Because I know I wouldn't live long enough to draw the pension.'

I could feel me face go white!

'Don't worry, Specs.' Johnny Merry was all cocky. 'He's only trying to scare us. He don't bother me.'

Well, he was bothering me alright, I can tell you.

Johnny was rocking his head now like Pretty Boy Romano did in the film.

'You know what my motto is,' he told the boxer. 'Live fast. Die young. And have a good-looking corpse.'

'Well, you'll be living fast and dying young alright,' the boxer told him. 'But I should forget the bit about having a good-looking corpse. When Killer Diller's finished with you, you'll be a very ugly corpse.'

Me mouth went as dry as a bone! To tell you the truth, if I'd been on me own then, I'd have legged it out of the fairground just as fast as I could.

Another boxer come in and we had boxing gloves laced on our hands, and we had to strip to our waists, and take our shoes off because we wasn't allowed to get into the ring wearing them.

'I like your shoes,' the boxer told Johnny. 'Can I have them?'

'You what?' Johnny looked all scornful.

'Well, you won't be needing 'um again, my buck. Because Killer Diller is feeling very, very nasty tonight. He's not going to be satisfied with just knocking you out. He's going to slaughter you.' The other boxer was looking at my shoes, but he only said, 'I don't think I'll bother trying these on. They're a bit too old and cheap. I'll just give them to charity.'

I'll tell you what, I was praying that a thunderbolt or something would hit the tent and stop the programme before I got into the ring.

But Johnny wasn't a bit scared. He just did his Pretty Boy Romano laugh, and told them, 'You wouldn't fancy making a little bet, would you? I reckon I'll knock Killer Diller out in the first round.'

The boxers just curled up laughing then, with their arms wrapped around each other and the tears running down their faces.

'Which one of us shall go first then, Specs?' Johnny asked me. 'Do you want me to?'

I didn't want to go first or second. I didn't want to go at all. But then all of a sudden I thought of the Foreign Legionnaires marching to Fort Zinderneuf, and it was ever so weird, but I started to feel all excited because I was having a real adventure at last, just like they'd had.

The crowd was all shouting inside the tent now, and singing, 'Why are we waiting?'

And like Beau Geste I said, 'I'll go first, mon ami. Them Tuaregs don't frighten me.'

'Toerags? Who the bleedin' hell is Toerags?' The boxers was looking at me like I was Doolally Tap. 'Youm fighting Mauler Malloy, not that geezer Toerags, whoever he might be. Now come on, let's have you inside.'

When we went inside the big tent

everybody cheered, but when I got up into the ring a bloke shouted, 'Just keep turning sideways, Specs, he won't be able to see you then.' And they all roared with laughing.

But I don't think that was funny. It's not my fault I'm a bit skinny, is it.

Mauler Malloy had ginger hair and big muscles and he didn't half look tough.

But do you know something? I didn't feel scared any more. I kept on thinking about Beau Geste and that I was having a real adventure, and I thought how great it 'ud be when I knocked Mauler Malloy out and won ten pounds. Glenda Shortway 'ud fall in love with me then, 'udden't she. I'd be a real hero at last.

The boss called us both to the centre of the ring and shouted a lot of stuff, but I didn't really hear what he was saying, because I could see meself in Foreign Legion uniform riding across the desert on a big black stallion, and Glenda Shortway was sitting on the horse in front of me with her arms wrapped around me neck.

Then I heard a bell ring, and the next thing I knew was that I was drowning!

'Go easy with that bloody water,' I could hear the boss saying. 'You'll wash the young sod down the drain else.'

Then *splash,* another lot of water come down on me head, and when I opened me eyes I was laying on the ground and there was a sort of blur of faces over me.

'He's opened his eyes, Boss,' one of them said.

'Thank Christ for that!' The boss sounded really relieved. 'I was beginning to think that you'd bloody well killed him, Mauler, and I'd have to pay for his funeral.'

'Don't talk so daft. I only tapped him.'

'Shove his glasses on,' somebody said, and then me glasses slid over me nose and I could see the boss and the boxers was all staring down at me.

Then I saw that there was somebody else laying at the side of me, and when I looked it was Johnny Merry. He was awake though, but he was rubbing the back of his head and cussing about how much it hurt.

'What happened to me?' I asked Johnny Merry.

'When the bell rang he knocked you out, Specs. It was over as quick as that. You looked like you was in a dream when you got into the ring.'

Me head was aching something cruel, and me jaw was swelling up as well, and it didn't half hurt when I touched it.

'Right then, they'm both alive so let's get the show back on the road. We got to put another couple of programmes on before the night ends, or else we'll be on poor street,' the boss said.

'Hold on a minute,' Johnny said. 'What about me money?'

'Money? What money?' The boss looked all shocked.

'I lasted three rounds,' Johnny said. 'I'm supposed to win five pounds for that.'

'You only lasted three rounds because you was running so fast Killer Diller couldn't catch you. So it warn't a boxing match, was it. It was a long distance race, and I don't pay any money for races.'

'What d'you call this, Scotch Mist?' Johnny showed him the lump on the back of his head.

'That was where the bottle hit you the three hundred and thirty-third time you passed the post in the last round, you young sod. Youm lucky you got out of the ring alive. The crowd would have lynched you if we hadn't stopped 'um. This four-eyed little git did better than you. At least he showed a bit of guts. He was facing the Mauler when he got knocked out, not running away like you was.'

They all left us then.

To tell you the truth, even though me head was aching and me jaw was hurting I felt chuffed when the boss said that I'd showed a bit of guts.

The gang was waiting for us, Terry Murtagh and Fatty Polson and Billy Green and Bokker Duggan. That's a funny name aren't it, Bokker. He hasn't got a Mam because she run off with a Yank in the war, and he lives with his Gran because his Dad is in prison for thieving. Me Mam always says that Bokker was born to hang because he comes from bad stock, but he's ever such a good bloke when you get to know him. Mind you, she always says the same thing about Johnny Merry. In fact as long as I can remember everybody has been saying that Johnny Merry was born to hang. It's funny because Terry Murtagh's dad, Ivor, is always getting put in prison but nobody ever says that Terry was born to hang.

'Why didn't you duck, Specs?' Fatty Polson asked me, all sneery. 'You should have kept your glasses on, you might have seen it coming then.'

'Because he's got guts and he wasn't scared, that's why he didn't duck,' Johnny Merry told him.

'Ah, but he aren't such a good runner as you, is he, Johnny. The other bloke would have caught him up, wouldn't he.'

Sometimes I think that Fatty Polson don't really like me or Johnny you know, because he's always having little digs at us. But then if we get narked about it, because it can get you narked sometimes, Fatty Polson always says he was only kidding.

'Did they give you any money?' Terry Murtagh wants to know.

'Money?' Johnny did his Pretty Boy Romano impression then. 'You mean dough? Okay? Who needs dough? Nick Romano don't fight for dough. Okay? Nick Romano just wanted to teach the punk a lesson he'd never forget. Okay! So don't let's hear any more malarky about dough. Okay! Let's just live fast, die young, and have a good-looking corpse. Okay?'

'Well, what shall we do now then?' Bokker Duggan was looking all fed up. 'If we got no dough we can't do nothing, can we.'

'We'll just have a mooch about,' Johnny

told him. 'And see what turns up.'

But to be honest, I was feeling all stiff and sore by then, and me head warn't half aching bad from being knocked out, so I said I was going home and I left them to it.

I was walking by meself and then Georgie Snood had to show up, didn't he. With his missus and a crowd of other blokes from the pub and their missuses. As soon as he saw me he started shouting, 'Take cover, everybody! Here comes Battling Specs, the Terror of the Boxing Booths. The One Punch Wonder. The other bloke throws a punch and Battling Specs moves like lightning and catches it straight on his chin.'

I just ignored him. I don't like him at all, you know.

Fifteen

We went poaching last night. It was Johnny Merry's idea. He said that an old bloke where he worked had been telling him about poaching, and how you could make a lot of money doing it, and eat some nice things as well. But I knew all about poaching before Johnny was talking about it. I got a book from the library about Poachers and Gamekeepers. In the book it said that the poachers was all evil criminals, stealing from the good people who owned the land. But when I asked Mr Sambourn about it, he told me that the book was just propaganda written at the behest of greedy and unscrupulous landowners, who forbade the poor even the chance to fill their empty bellies with what a bounteous nature had created for all men to enjoy ...

It's great the way that Mr. Sambourn talks, aren't it: 'propaganda written at the behest of greedy and unscrupulous landowners who forbade the poor even the chance to fill their empty bellies with what a bounteous nature had created for all men to enjoy ...' I wish I could say things like that.

There's lots of places to go poaching round here because there's a lot of farms all around the town, and there's a big estate as well owned by Lord Ragstone. I've seen him a few times driving down the town in a big old Rolls Royce. He always wears one of those Deerstalker hats on his head, and plus-fours trousers. When I was a kid I always used to think that all Lords and Ladies were descended from the knights who used to fight at tournaments and go on Crusades, but Mr Sambourn told me that only a few Lords and Ladies were descended from the knights. He says that most of them nowadays are descended from brewers and political hacks and people who spent their lives exploiting and cheating the poor. And he says that a lot of them are descended from women who used to sleep with the olden-time Kings, and got their titles for giving the King what he wanted in bed.

When I told me Mam what he'd said, she just sniffed. 'Well then, Doreen Merry has been wasting her time sleeping with all them bloody Yanks and Poles and Blackies in the war, and the bloody councillors she's knocked off since. She ought to have gone to London instead and met the King. She'd have been Lady Muck by now.'

The reason me Mam's being nasty about Doreen Merry is because they've fallen out again. They're always doing that, falling out and making up. This time they've fallen out over Sid. Me Mam said that

Doreen was making eyes at him, and Doreen told her that she'd sooner make eyes at a bloody mackerel.

'And you'd do that if there warn't any men around.' Me Mam was all scornful. 'Because some of the bloody men you've been with 'ud make a mackerel look like a good catch.'

'Oooohhhh, you can talk, you can!' Doreen put on her superior look then. She says that when she puts on her superior look she shrivels her enemies up. 'Just look at you now, Effie Kensal, living with two blokes, and if you put the two of 'um together they 'udden't be able to make a real man's donger, not if they was joined together and your brother Harold's donger give to 'um as well. A bloody dead mackerel 'ud be a real good catch compared to the sort of blokes you've only ever managed to have. Mind you, I expect they thinks they're in bed with a fish anyway, when they're in bed with you.'

Me Mam went mental. 'What do you mean by that, Doreen Merry?' she hissed all deadly.

'Eggzackly what I says, Effie Kensal,' Doreen told her, all contemptuous. 'If the smell fits, then wear it. That's what I always says.'

They started fighting then, and a bloke who was walking up the street jumped in between them to stop the fight. When he did that they both set about him instead. They was skreeking at him, 'Mind your own business, you. Who does you think you am? Gerron back down to your own street and keep your nose out of our business.'

They didn't half give him a good hiding.

He had stopped the fight though, because when they'd finished with him they was both too knackered to keep on fighting each other. But they're still not speaking yet.

To tell you the truth me Mam embarrasses me sometimes. I mean, you don't expect your mother to fight in the street like a tearaway, do you. Fighting's alright for blokes, but it's not really very nice when women do it, is it. What I don't like about it the most is that it gives stuck-up cows like Mrs Jones-Evans the chance to stick her nose up at people like us, don't it. Ever since I was a little kid I've heard her going on about the roughs and scruffs she lives by, and when me Mam fights in the street then it makes me wonder sometimes if Mrs Jones Evans might have a bit of truth in what she keeps on saying about us.

Now what was I on about before. Oh yeah. Poaching.

Johnny Merry said that this old bloke had told him that the easiest way to poach pheasants and partridges and birds like that was to feed 'um with grain that had been soaked in whisky, or gin or rum. After the birds had ate a few grains they got so drunk that they just fell over and then you only had to pick 'um up and put 'um in a sack. Or he said you could wait until they'd gone to roost on the trees then spread some nets and scare the birds into them. Or if you had an air rifle you could easy go underneath the branches they were sleeping on, their bedroom like, and pick them off like a sniper.

The old bloke said that you could tickle trout in a stream, by slipping your hand under their bellies and stroking them nice and gentle, and then you had to move your fingers very slow up to the gills and suddenly flick them up onto the bank.

He said that for hares and rabbits you only needed snares, or ferrets and nets. We already knew about ferrets and nets and snares from when we was kids and we'd helped Fred Ferret and the Stargazer catch the rabbits down Mrs Jones-Evans's garden that time.

'What shall we go for then?' I asked Johnny Merry.

'Well, we haven't got any nets or ferrets, and we haven't got any whisky or gin or rum to soak grain in. We haven't got any grain anyway, have we. And I don't fancy lying down on a muddy bank with me arms in cold water, so I reckon we'll use an air rifle and snipe the birds. It'll be dead easy.' He was all smiles until he remembered that we hadn't got an air rifle neither.

'Fatty Polson's got an air rifle,' I remembered. His Dad had bought it for him ages ago.

We went to ask Fatty Polson to lend us the gun, but he wouldn't. Not unless he could come poaching with us as well. We didn't want to take him, so we was arguing with him and his Dad come out then and asked us what we was arguing about, and like a mug Fatty Polson told him.

'They wants to borrow me air rifle to go poaching with, Dad.'

I thought that his Dad would go mental

then, but he didn't. He just looked all crafty.

'Oh yes? Want to do a bit of poaching, do you? What was you thinking of poaching then?'

I can't take this in, you know. Why Mr Polson aren't going mental, I mean. He got religion a few months ago, you see, and now he's a big noise in the Baptist Chapel and spends all his Sundays singing hymns and calling on the Lord to redeem the wretched sinners. Only last week he reported a kid who was scrumping some sour apples from the Old Hostel gardens to the police. And that was nothing to do with him at all, was it. If the kid hadn't scrumped them sour cooking apples they'd have only fallen on the ground and rotted. And he keeps on reporting the kids to the police for playing football in the street.

But Johnny Merry took it in straight away. He don't miss nothing, he don't. He really is a City Slicker, aren't he.

'Well, we was going after pheasants, Mr Polson,' he said all polite. 'They're very tasty this time of year, you know.'

'So I believe.' Mr Polson nodded all wisely and started stroking some of his chins. He's got dozens of them hanging down under his chin in rolls. 'And what was you thinking of doing with these pheasants when you've catched them?'

'We're going to eat them. Except for the ones we gives to our friends.' Johnny winked at him.

'So if I was to lend you the gun, would I be one of them friends of yours?' Mr Polson wanted to know.

'I should say so,' Johnny told him. 'A nice pheasant would make a real good dinner for you tomorrow, wouldn't it, Mr Polson?'

'I don't reckon one 'ud be enough to fill my stomach, young Merry.'

Mr Polson's belly is massive! And I mean, massive!

'I reckon two might fill it though,' Johnny said.

'No, I reckon it 'ud take more than two.' Mr Polson was shaking his head and frowning all thoughtfully. 'I reckon it might take half a dozen to fill me right up.'

'Half a dozen it is then,' Johnny told him.

'Fetch that gun out here,' Mr Polson told Fatty.

'Ohhh Dadddd! I don't want to lend

it to ’um, unless they takes me with ’um.’ Fatty was pulling his face about and grumbling, until his dad didn’t half fetch him a crack across the earhole.

‘How dare you talk like that, you wretched sinner! Poaching thy neighbour’s chattels is a sin in the eyes of the Lord. Now fetch that gun out here.’

When we was walking away with the gun and a tin of pellets I asked Johnny, ‘Why can you catch on so quick to what people are really like, and I can’t?’

‘I dunno, Specs,’ he said. ‘But our Doreen reckons that you’re a bit simple-minded. Maybe that’s the reason.’

Do you know, I reckon he could be right about me being a bit simple-minded, because I must be to put up with all the aggravation I get at home.

Like when last week me Mam said that she was going to have to have more money off me for my bed and board. She said that it was because the cost of living was going up again, and I’d got to help to shoulder the burden. But I’d been giving her nearly all me money anyway, so I said to her, ‘Why can’t me Dad start shouldering a bit of the burden? He never pays a penny for his bed and board, does he. And he’s still sleeping on my campbed, as well. And the sofa is making me all crooked, because it's too short for me to stretch out on when I'm asleep.'

'Ohh, you unnatural savage!' she skreeked at me. 'How can you begrudge your darling Father a few bites to eat, and a place to lay his weary head, after all he's done for you?'

All me Dad's ever done for me is to run off and leave me when I was a babby. Mind you, thinking about it, I reckon he did me a good turn when he did that, because he's driving me up the wall now, so God only knows what I'd be like if he'd been living with us while I was growing up. I reckon I'd have been in the Funny Farm long ago, and that's a fact.

Anyway, in the end she nagged me so much that I did give her more money for me bed and board, even though it's leaving me nearly broke, which is why I've got to go poaching with Johnny Merry just to try and earn a few extra shillings.

Then the other day when I got in from work, I was starving hungry and the house was empty, and there was a note on the table that me Mam had left for me. It said:

'Dear Specs, I hope you've got some money to go and buy yourself some fish and chips for your supper, because if you haven't then you'll have to kill the cat and eat it.'

It aren't fair, is it!

Well, as soon as we got the air rifle me and Johnny Merry got on our bikes and we went to some woods that Lord Ragstone owns.

Now the old bloke had told Johnny that the best time to shoot the pheasants was when it got dark and they was all asleep in their bedroom. All you had to do was to take a torch and shine the light into their eyes. Then even if they wakes up it doesn't matter because they're all dazzled and dazed by the light, and they still stays sitting on the branches in their bedroom so you can shoot them very easily.

So we hid our bikes and we lay down under some bushes to wait for it to get dark. We was having a smoke and a laugh, and I was thinking how great it was. It was an adventure really, wasn't it. It was just like that book I'd read about the poachers and gamekeepers in the olden days. I kept thinking to meself ...

'My name is Beau Specs, and I'm the leader of a desperate gang of poachers, and we're going to take hundreds and hundreds of pheasants from the lands of the wicked tyrant, Lord Ragstone, to feed the poor starving hungry women and children with. I'll lead my desperate gang through Hell and High Water and fight a thousand of Lord Ragstone's bloodthirsty gamekeepers if I have to.'

Then it got dark and we started to creep through the woods looking for the pheasants' bedroom.

It was great! It was really exciting! I reckon it was nearly as exciting as being a Foreign Legionnaire marching to Fort Zinderneuf.

But after a long while, when we still hadn't found the pheasants' bedroom it started to get a bit boring. And I fell over dead logs a few times, and cut me knee and tore all me trousers, and once me glasses fell off and it took us ages to find them again, because we couldn't shine the torch in case the gamekeepers was hiding in the trees watching for us.

You see, what we'd decided was that we'd wait until we found the pheasants before we used the torch. That way, even if the gamekeepers saw the fight flashing we'd still have time enough to shoot a lot of pheasants and get away before the gamekeepers could reach us.

Then it started to rain.

I was feeling really miserable and me knee was hurting where I'd cut it, and it wasn't like an adventure anymore. I wanted to pack it in and go home, but I wouldn't say that to Johnny Merry because if I did he'd only think that I was a wimp.

We kept on wandering around in the dark and the wet, and then Johnny said, 'Does you know where we are, Specs?'

'No,' I told him. 'I thought you did.'

'Well, I thought you did. Because you never said nothing about us being lost, did you.' He sounded all narked and miserable. 'How are we going to find the pheasants' bedroom if we're lost? And how are we going to find our way out of these woods? And how are we going to find our bikes?'

Listening to his moaning cheered me up, you know. Because he sounded as miserable and fed up as I was feeling. So I wasn't such a wimp after all, was I.

'Bugger this for a game of soldiers, Specs. Let's go back home, shall we. Have you got any idea which way to go?'

'No, Johnny. I aren't got the foggiest.' To tell the truth I got a bit scared then, because I could just imagine us wandering around in these woods all night, and perhaps even dying from the cold and wet.

And then I got really scared, because we heard a voice!

Yeah. It's true. We was right in the middle of these woods, miles from anywhere in the pitch dark, and we heard a voice!

I was shivering because I thought it might be a ghost or a demon, and Johnny Merry was as scared as me, because he pushed right in close to me under the same bush I was hiding under and I could feel him shaking and shivering as well.

The voice kept coming closer and closer, and I was getting scareder and scareder, and when the voice got really close I suddenly heard what it was saying.

' ... Now listen carefully, because I shall not repeat this again. I'm sick and tired of you arguing this point with me. I say again: the four principal feet found in English poetry are the iambic, the trochaic, the dactylic and the anapestic. This has been established since the fourteenth century. Geoffrey Chaucer provides fine examples of it in his work ... So, what do you say to that?'

When I heard this I was so relieved that I nearly fainted.

'It's bloody Stargazer!' Johnny Merry didn't half sound glad, I'll tell you.

But I don't think he was half so glad as I was.

The Stargazer is one of the town's nut-cases. He walks around all day and night talking to the sky. He never looks at the ground at all. Even when he's having something to eat or drink, he still keeps on talking all the time to the sky.

'We can shine the torch,' Johnny said. 'Because if Stargazer's here, then Fred Ferret must be somewhere around here as well. So there won't be any gamekeepers about, will there.'

Fred Ferret is the craftiest poacher and rabbit-catcher in the whole of England, and he always takes Stargazer around with him to carry the pheasants and rabbits and pigeons he catches. So he'd got to be close to us.

I was really pleased to think that Fred Ferret was somewhere about, because he could show us the way out of the woods, and that's all I wanted to do. Just to get out from these rotten cold wet woods. I didn't want to be a poacher any more. Let somebody else steal the wicked tyrant Lord Ragstone's pheasants and feed the starving hungry women and kids of the poor. All I wanted was to get home and get warm and dry again.

Johnny shone the torch on Stargazer, but Stargazer just went on talking to the sky.

'... non-metrical prosody is a feature of modern poetry, although many critics may deny that it is impossible to write poetry without employing some kind of metre. I can state with absolute authority that visual prosodies have been fostered by poets of the Imagist Movement ...'

You should have seen the state of Stargazer. He was wearing an old army beret with some feathers stuck into it, and a Scotchman's kilt, and a pair of wellies. I hadn't seen him in any of them before. God only knows where he got them from. But he was still wearing his Mam's old pink coat that he's always wore for as long as I've known him, and the mangy old fox fur with a real head and glass eyes wrapped round his neck.

'Where's Freddy?' I kept on asking Stargazer, but he never took a blind bit of notice of me.

'... of course e.e.cummings has recently revived the practice of some Metaphysical poets in shaping the verse by typographical arrangement ...'

Then this massive big dog come out from the dark, growling and snarling at us.

I wasn't scared because I knew it was only Ivan Ferret, Fred Ferret's dog. Everybody calls him the Hound of the Baskervilles because he's so fierce-looking and massive and a lot of them are scared of him, but he's as daft as a brush really. He wouldn't hurt a fly.

'Shut your rattle, Ivan,' I told him, and he started wagging his tail and jumping up trying to lick me.

When I was a kid Fred Ferret had a dog named Edgar Ferret who was really crafty. It used to run round all the butchers' shops pinching sausages and pork pies and meat and taking them home for Fred Ferret to eat.

Then one day Edgar disappeared, but a kid I know told me that he'd seen Edgar going into Mr Solomon's butchers shop, but he never saw Edgar come out again. And the very next day there was a big tray of meat pies in Mr Solomon's window with a sign on them saying, 'Fresh made from local animals'.

Ever since then Mr Solomon's nickname has been 'Sweeney Dog'.

Anyway, the next thing I knew Fred Ferret was standing straight in front of me, and I hadn't neither heard nor seen him coming, you know. He's like a shadow the way he moves. No wonder he catches so many rabbits. I mean to say, if Big City Slickers like me and Johnny Merry can't hear or see him coming, what chance do rabbits have? They're only yokels, aren't they. Dead slow-thinking compared to us.

Fred Ferret is called Fred Ferret because he looks like a ferret. He wears a great big floppy cap and a baggy coat with a lot of hidden pockets to put the stuff that he's pinched in. And he wears old-fashioned leather gaiters and britches. And his face is all scrunched up and tiny under his cap and he twitches his whiskers like a ferret does, especially when he's talking to you. He's got thousands of ferrets, you know. He carries them in his pockets and under his cap, and they runs about all over his house. Do you know that you never see a cat or any other dog except Ivan Ferret within a three-mile circle of Fred Ferret's house, because they're all too scared to come there because of his ferrets.

'Ahrrr Ahrrr Ahrrr?' he asked me.

'We come to poach some pheasants, Fred,' I told him.

'Ahrrr Ahrrrr Ahrrr Ahrrr!' He was ever so fierce.

'There's no need to get mad at us, Fred. We didn't know that you was coming here tonight, did we,' I said ever so nice.

'Ahrrr? Ahrrr.' He calmed down a bit.

A lot of people don't know what Fred Ferret is on about when he talks, you know. Because he only ever says that one thing: 'Ahrrr'.

But he's ever so easy to understand once you get to know him.

So I asked him how we could get back to where we'd left our bikes.

'Ahrrr Ahrrr Ahrrr.' He pointed. 'Ahrrr Ahrrr ... Ahrrr.'

'Thanks, Fred.' I was really grateful, I'll tell you, because I was dead sick of them woods.

'Ahrrr Ahrrr.' He pulled a couple of dead pheasants from out of his jacket and give them to me.

'Corrr, thanks ever so much, Fred,' we both told him.

'Ahrrr Ahrrr Ahrrrr Ahrrr Ahrrr.' He was all smiling now.

'Tarra Fred, Tarra Ivan, Tarra Stargazer.' We started off down the track Fred had showed us.

'Ahrrr Ahrrr,' Fred said.

'Wooff woof woof,' daft Ivan told us.

' ... do you dispute my statement that the prosody of Latin and Greek poetry was determined by quantitative metres. This was possible because the rules governing length of vowels, i.e. quantity, were established by precise grammatical conventions,' Stargazer told the sky, and he was grinning all smug at it because he knew he'd won this argument and had got the sky beat.

'Shall we give one of these pheasants to Mr Polson?' I asked Johnny Merry.

'Bugger Mr Polson.' Johnny was all smiles now. 'We'll cook 'um and eat 'um ourselves. I reckon we've earned 'um after traipsing round these bloody woods all night like this.'

He was right, you know.

The track we was on seemed to go round and round in circles a lot, and it took us ages to get out of the woods. When we got to the road we knew where we were, so we went to get our bikes, only when we got to the place where we'd hid them, they was gone.

And just as we found out that our bikes had gone, a bloke come out from the trees pointing a shotgun at us, and there was a copper with him.

'Stand still or I'll blow your bloody yeds off.' The bloke sounded like he meant it as well, so we just stood rock still.

'I'll take them.' He snatched the pheasants from me, and then the copper said, 'And I'll take that.' And he snatched the air rifle off Johnny Merry.

'You're both under arrest for poaching,' the copper told us.

'Oh God!' I felt me heart drop right down into me boots, you know. Because me Mam is going to kill me when she finds out about this.

'What about our bikes?' Johnny warn't a bit bothered about being arrested for poaching.

Well, it's alright for him, aren't it. He only lives with his sister Doreen, and she don't give a bugger what he gets up to. Not like me Mam with me.

'What bikes?' The copper acted all puzzled. 'Has you seen any bikes, Mr Frinton?'

The bloke with the shotgun just laughed all sneery-like. 'I haven't seen any bikes, Constable Jones.'

'You've pinched 'um.' Johnny was getting really mad, I could see that. And I was feeling mad now, as well, because the way that copper and that Frinton bloke was acting you could see that they did know something about our bikes.

Quick as a flash the copper handcuffed me and Johnny together and him and Frinton dragged us off down the road to where the police van was waiting with another copper driving it.

'Here we are then,' Jones told him all grinning. 'We've captured Robin Hood and Little John tonight.'

And all three of 'um roared with laughing.

Oh, very funny, I don't think.

Anyway, at the Police Station the sergeant took our names and addresses and he bailed us until next week. He said we'd be notified when we had to appear in the magistrate's court.

'What'll happen to us?' I asked him.

'You'll get seven to ten years Hard Labour for this, I should think,' he said, and all the coppers and that bloke Frinton all roared with laughing.

Oh, very funny, I don't think.

Johnny reckons we'll only get a telling off, and a fine.

I'm not so worried about that. But what am I going to tell me Mam when she wants to know where me bike is? And what am I going to tell her when she finds out that I've got to go to the magistrate's court? And what about Fatty Polson's air rifle? What's his dad going to do when he finds out that the police have got it?

I wish I'd never read that rotten book about Poachers and Gamekeepers, you know.

Sixteen

I got up real early to go to work today because I didn't want me Mam to see that I hadn't got me bike. So I got out of the house before anybody else had woke up.

At least that was what I thought, but when I was walking to work who should I meet but Uncle Harold all dressed up in his top hat and cloak. He was standing in the Recreation Garden down town, staring at the fountain. I don't know why because it still hasn't got no water coming out of it.

I had to find out what he was doing there so early in the morning, because Uncle Harold don't like getting up early, you know.

When he saw me he said, 'Good Morrow, Specs. Well met. What brings you wandering abroad at such an early hour of this shining morn?'

He's been talking funny like this ever since he got up again after his last nervous breakdown. The one he had when Smiling

Sam give him the sack.

Oh, I forgot to tell you that he's forgiven me for what happened to his 'Sweet Dreams Mobile Resting Haven'. When he got up again he said that he realised that it wasn't completely my fault, and that we could be friends again.

I know that it wasn't any of my fault at all, what happened. But I don't like not being friends with Uncle Harold, so I said alright and didn't bother to keep on arguing the toss about it.

'I'm going to work, Uncle Harold,' I told him.

'Ah yes. Work. It is a blessed thing, Specs, is work. Every man should have his work to go to. The man who does not have work is a man who is leading a shallow and empty and worthless existence. Work is noble, Specs.'

I can't take this in, you know. Hearing Uncle Harold going on about work like this. I mean, he hates work, don't he! Ever since I can remember he's never done any proper work at all.

'Well, what are you doing here, Uncle Harold?" I ask him.

'I am contemplating my life, Specs. I am trying to seek direction. I am endeavouring to ascertain to what purpose I may utilise my myriad talents.'

To be honest I'm finding this all a bit too much at this time of a morning.

'Well, I'll have to go, Uncle Harold. I've got to get to work.'

'Wait a moment more, my dear Specs.' He threw out his arms all dramatic-like. 'I just want to say a heartfelt thank you for saving my life as you have.'

Saving his life? He's starting to give me the creeps now.

'How have I saved your life, Uncle Harold?' I asked him.

'Because if you hadn't come to me at this opportune moment, Specs, it would have been too late. I was about to cast myself into the depths. I was about to drown myself, Specs.'

'Drown yourself? Where?'

'There,' he told me, and pointed at the fountain pool. 'I was going to cast myself into the waters of Lethe.'

'But there's no water in that pool, Uncle Harold,' I told him. 'So how was you going to manage to drown yourself in it?'

He smiled all sort of pitying at me. 'Figuratively, my dear boy. Figuratively.'

The church clock started striking then,

and all I could think of to say was, 'Greasy Joe's cafe 'ull be open now, Uncle Harold. Why don't you go and have a cup of tea and a bacon butty. You'll feel a lot better then.'

'Indeed I shall, Specs. Indeed I shall.' He sort of threw his cloak around him and went stalking off towards Greasy Joe's cafe.

It's no wonder I'm half-daft, is it! Not with the family I've got!

When I got to work I went into the Stores Office where all the Fitters and Mates have to meet first thing to see what jobs they're being sent on. As soon as I walked through the door there was a massive cheer went up.

Georgie Snood shouted, 'Welcome, Nimrod. Mighty Hunter before the Lord!'

I just stood there, and then he shouted, 'Close your mouth, Nimrod, you'se caught enough flies for this morning already. The species is in danger of being exterminated.'

'Lord Ragstone is going to demand the Death Penalty,' another of the Fitters shouted, and everybody was roaring with laughing at me, and I could feel meself turning bright red.

'Has you brought your bow and arrow with you today, Robin?'

'The people down Martlin Street says could you go down there right away because there's a man-eating lion on the prowl.'

'And a bloke from Brummagem wants to know if you got any tiger skins for sale.'

It's true what they say about this town, you know. Everybody reckons that if a fly is going to fart at the top end of the town, then everybody down the bottom end smells the stink before the fly's even farted.

'When are you up in front of the beaks then, Nimrod?' Georgie Snood was loving it because I was in trouble.

'It's none of your business.' I got a bit narked with him then.

'Oh, excuse me, Nimrod, but it is my business. And it's the business of every law-abiding citizen of this town when armed gangs of criminals am running wild about the countryside, what do you say, Chaps?'

Of course they all agreed with him, didn't they.

And then Mr Thrall poked his head out from his office door and shouted,

'Kensal, I want a word with you. Get in here now.'

All the Fitters and mates started nudging each other and grinning, and whispering to me when I went past them.

'Youm for it now.'

'You're getting the chop.'

'Good riddance.'

'You'll never make a Gas Fitter not so long as you've got a'nole in your arse.'

'Goodbye, Nimrod.'

There's one of the Mates that I can't stand, you know. His name's John Taylor, and his uncle is a copper. He's about a year older than me, and he comes to work every day in a clean pair of overalls, and a clean white shirt and tie, and he's a proper Mammy's Darling. And he's a real snide. Always carrying tales and trying to get other lads into trouble. When we was at school he never ever got into trouble with the teachers, and never got mucky or anything like the rest of us. Of course all the Fitters reckons that he's a wonderful mate, because he loves being on the Gas. He loves making joints and screwing pipes and he don't want any adventures at all. He says that he likes living with his Mam. because she looks after him and makes him all comfortable, and when I told him one day that I was going to join the Foreign Legion, he just stared at me like I was mental.

I reckon Glenda Shortway likes him a bit, you know. Because when we're at the Youth Club she's always talking to him. I can't see what she wants to talk to him for, I really can't.

When I went past him to go into Mr Thrall's office, he grinned all sneery-like, and all of a sudden I knew! I knew who'd told everybody about me being caught poaching. It must have been his uncle, the copper, who told John Taylor, and he'd come rushing to work to tell everybody else.

'It was you, warn't it?' I said. 'You told everybody about me and Johnny Merry, didn't you?'

'It just serves you right, Specs Kensal.' He's got a horrible voice, you know. He talks through his nose. 'I hope Mr Thrall sacks you now. You're not Gas Fitter material, you're not.'

I was trying to think of something really cool and City Slicker to say to him, but then Mr Thrall shouted, 'I shan't tell you again, Kensal. Get in here!'

To tell you the truth I was feeling a bit scared now. Even though I hates being on the Gas, I'm still scared of getting the sack, because God only knows what me Mam would do to me.

Anyway, I didn't get it, did I.

You're not going to believe what happened when I got into Mr Thrall's office.

'Close the door,' he said. 'And stand there where I can see you.'

He was sitting behind his desk, staring ever so close at me. He's got one of them faces like that bloke on the wireless sings about. You know that song, don't you ...

'I'm a bodyguard of Julius Caesar,
Got a face like a lemon squeezer ...'

Well that's just what Mr Thrall's face is like. All long-nosed and pointy and sour.

'In trouble with the police, are you, Kensal?' he said. 'What's your Mam have to say about it? Going mental, is she?'

He knows me Mam, you see.

'She don't know yet,' I told him.

'Oh, don't she. Well now, I know what she'll say when she finds out, Kensal. She'll go mental, won't she.'

I just nodded.

'And what'll she say if I sacks you because you're in trouble with the police, Kensal?'

'She'll go double-mental, Mr Thrall,' I told him.

Do you know, I was beginning to think that there was something funny going on here. Because if he was going to sack me, then he was going a long way around the houses to do it, wasn't he.

He sat there humming and aarrhhing for a bit, examining his fingernails ever so close. Then he looked straight at me and told me, 'All the Fitters say that you're bloody useless on the job, Kensal. They all says that you've got no interest in it. What have you got to say about that?'

Well, there wasn't much I could say about that, was there. I mean, it was true, wasn't it. So I didn't say anything.

Then he asked me, 'How would you feel if I give you the sack now?'

I thought about that for a bit. Because to tell you the truth I didn't really know how I'd feel. It was like there was different voices in me head telling me it would be great if he sacked me, and it would be awful if he sacked me.

I can't take it in, the way he's going on. He's making me feel all mixed up.

I was wishing that Mr Sambourn was here, because he'd be able to explain to me exactly what was going on.

'All the Fitters want me to give you the sack, you know, Kensal,' he said next; and all of a sudden a voice in me head told me ever so loud, 'Tell him to shove the bloody job up his Jacksy, Specs.'

And the voice was so strong that I opened me mouth to tell Mr Thrall that, but before I could he told me ever so quick, 'But I'm not going to sack you, my boy. I'm going to give you another chance.'

I was so surprised I shut me mouth again.

'But ...' He grinned all snidey now. 'You've got to do me a favour, because I'm doing you one, aren't I?'

I felt a bit wary when he said that. I wondered if he was one of them dirty old men, to be honest. But then I thought of Johnny Merry always telling me, 'Box clever, Specs. Box clever.'

'What sort of favour, Mr Thrall?' I heard me voice saying. Honest! I hadn't thought of saying that. It just seemed to come out of its own accord.

'Oh, just keep your eyes peeled and your ears open,' he said all casual-like. 'And tell me on the quiet what the Fitters are getting up to when my back's turned. It'll be our secret, Kensal. Just between you, me and the gatepost.'

Do you know I thought again of Johnny Merry telling me, 'Box clever, Specs. Box clever.' So I just said, 'Alright, Mr Thrall.'

'Right.' He got all abrupt then. 'Just remember, this is our secret. Say nothing to nobody about it. Off you go.'

Aren't there a lot of snidey rotten people in this world!

Mr Sambourn always says that a real man acts with honour, and tells people to their faces what he thinks of them, but never goes behind their backs.

Mr Sambourn's right, because in all the books I've read Beau Geste and Beau Sabreur and Sinbad the Soldier never goes behind people's backs to get them into trouble. They always stands and tells them to their faces what they thinks of them. Mind you, I think that you have to be a bit careful about telling some people to their faces, because they might turn round and give you a good hiding. So I think you have to box a bit clever with that one. But anyway, no matter what I'd told him, I wasn't going to start carrying tales about the Fitters and Mates to Mr Thrall. Even though I knew that there was some of the Fitters and Mates who carried tales to him about me.

When I come out of Mr Thrall's office everybody was staring at me, but I never looked at any of them. I just went and stood at the end of the counter by meself. They started whispering to each other, and then Georgie Snood come up to me.

'Well?' he said.

I didn't say nothing.

'Has he sacked you?' he asked me.

I didn't look at him, but just shook me head. Then I squinted at him out of the corner of me eye, all sly-like.

I could see him looking all puzzled at the others.

Then he asked me, 'What did he say to you then?'

I don't know what made me do what I did then. It just seemed to come over me all of a sudden. But I turned round and looked him straight in the face and said very quiet, 'Mr Thrall and me have come to an arrangement.'

Then I shut up, and do you know something, it was as if for the first time in me life I was really taking it all in. I was looking at Georgie Snood's face and it was just like I could read it like a book. It was really weird, because it was like even though I couldn't understand all the words I could still understand exactly what the book was telling me. And what it was telling me was that Georgie Snood and the rest of them had tried to get me the sack when they went rushing to tell Mr Thrall that I was in trouble with the police for poaching, but that their plan had backfired on them, and now they was worried to death because they didn't know what the agreement between Mr Thrall and me that I'd just told Georgie Snood about, might be. But that what I'd just told Snoodie had put the boot on the other foot, and I was wearing it now.

I never said a word all the morning, just did whatever Georgie Snood told me to do, and he was trying to be ever so nice and smarmy as well.

Then, as soon as it was dinnertime I run round to Mr Sambourn's house to tell him all about what was happening.

He listened very careful to everything I told him, and then he roared with laughing.

'It appears that you've hoisted your workmates with their own petard, Specs.'

I had to ask him what a petard was ...

Seventeen

When I was walking back from work tonight Johnny Merry come running up behind me.

'Guess what I've just seen, Specs. Bloody Stargazer riding like the clappers down Front Hill.'

I couldn't see what Johnny was getting so excited about. A lot of people ride like the clappers down Front Hill.

'It was my bike he was riding on, Specs.'

I'll tell you what, it only took me a couple of seconds to take this in, you know.

'Bloody Fred Ferret has done us, Johnny. It was him who pinched our bikes, and he give us them pheasants so the coppers would nab us with them. He must have sent for the coppers while we was wandering around on that long path he sent us on.'

It's weird, aren't it. How I'm taking everything in today. Georgie Snood, John Taylor, Mr Thrall, and now Fred Ferret. It's like me brain has suddenly woke up.

Johnny Merry was staring at me like he didn't know me.

'Blimey Specs,' he said. 'Youm starting to think like a real City Slicker.'

I felt really chuffed when he told me that.

'What shall we do, Specs?' Johnny asked me.

I had to think about about that one. Because it wasn't very often that Johnny ever asked me what we ought to do about something. In fact, I don't think he'd asked me since we was little kids. And I had a job remembering when he'd asked me then.

Then I remembered one of them cool things that Pretty Boy Romano had said in the picture. So I said it as well.

'It's pay-back time, Johnny. Fred Ferret don't know just who he's tangling with, does he. So let's show him.'

We went down to Fred Ferret's house

and had a sneak around it to see if we could see my bike. Because if Stargazer had Johnny's bike, then it was more than likely that Fred Ferret had kept mine, wasn't it.

The trouble was that Fred Ferret lives in the middle of a row of houses right on the street without any front gardens or anything, and you can only get to the back of the houses by going down the entry at one end of the row. At the back there's a long narrow yard and some old wash houses built up against a factory wall, and all the back windows of the houses opens onto the yard, so it's a bit hard to try and sneak around the back yard because everybody can see you if they just looks out of their windows.

When we went down the entry and round the corner the first house we passed there was an old woman sitting looking out of the window, and she come skreeking out.

'What's you want? Who're you? What's you doing sneaking about round here?'

She looked just like one of them witches in the fairy stories, all bent and twisted and scruffy with her hair all flying out round her head.

Johnny did his Pretty Boy Romano imitation.

'Stay cool, Baby. Live fast, die young, and have a good-looking corpse.'

'You cheeky young devils. I'll bloody well cool you.' she skreeked, and she run back into her house and next second come roaring out again with an axe. 'Never mind cool you, I'll bleedin' well crown you. I'll make you into corpses.'

I'll tell you what, if I hadn't ducked she'd have chopped me head off with the first swing. But I was ever so fast and the axe missed me and broke the window instead.

Then all the rest of the neighbours come boiling out into the yard. And they was all shouting and bawling, 'Kill! Kill! Kill!'

At least, that's what it sounded like they was bawling.

All me and Johnny could do was to skedaddle back up the entry as fast as we could and get out of that street before they lynched us.

When I got me breath back I told Johnny, 'We'll come back tonight. Fred Ferret 'ull be out poaching then, won't he. When it's dark nobody can see us so we can get into his house and have a good look around for me bike.'

It's amazing! It's like a miracle! I'm thinking like a real City Slicker! Do you know, Georgie Snood said to me one day that I was like a room which had the light on, but there was nobody inside it. And now look at me. The light's blazing, and I'm inside the room.

When I got home me Mam wanted to know where me bike was, so I told her it had a puncture and I'd left it at work. Then she nagged me for an hour and twenty-three minutes about anything she could think of until I managed to escape.

I went to call for Johnny Merry and Doreen, his big sister, answered the door.

'Hello, Beau Geste, wipe your feet before you comes in. I'm sick of sweeping sand up after you.'

She's always taking the mickey out of me because she knows that I'm going to join the Foreign Legion as soon as I've saved enough money for me passport and the fare to France.

As soon as I got into the house the first thing I saw was Johnny's bike.

'How did you get that back?' I asked him.

'He bloody well didn't get it back,' Doreen said. 'I bloody well got it back for him.'

She always swears all the time, Doreen does.

'I saw bloody Stargazer riding it down town, so I bloody well knocked him off it and brought it back here.'

She was glaring at me. 'And another bloody thing. I'se got a bloody bone to pick with you, Specs Kensal. What does you bloody mean by getting my brother into bloody trouble all the bloody time. I'se had a bloody 'nuff of it. He's not bloody well going out with you no more.'

I can't take this in, you know. I mean to say, Doreen has never ever cared what Johnny gets up to. And it's not me who gets Johnny into trouble. It's him who's always got me into trouble. So what's brought this on all of a sudden?

'Gerrout of my house!' she skreeked. 'And don't you bloody well come back here again.'

Before I could say a word she grabbed me and run me out of the house and slammed the door shut behind me.

I moped about a bit outside the door, and then the top bedroom window slid up and Johnny whispered down to me, ‘I’ll tell you all about it tomorrow, Specs. But I can’t come with you tonight.’

And he closed the window again before I could say anything.

I felt a bit miserable then, because I didn’t want to go to Fred Ferret’s house on me own, but then, all of a sudden, I thought, ‘My name is Beau Specs of the Legion. I don’t need anybody to help me to do anything. I’ll get me bike back by meself. Even if I have to go through Hell’s fires to get it.’

I felt like I was marching to Fort Zinderneuf when I went down town to Fred Ferret’s house.

The street was all quiet and dark, because somebody had broke the bulb in the lamp. I went sliding along on the opposite side of the road to Fred Ferret’s row. It was just like being a secret agent moving through the shadows. Fred Ferret’s house was all dark as well, and then I saw that the front downstairs window was open a bit.

To tell you the truth, I got a bit scared then. I’d never crept into anybody’s house before, you see. Except for me own. It would be like being a burglar, wouldn’t it. But then I thought, 'No! I'm not being a burglar, am I. Because I'm not going to pinch anything from Fred Ferret. All I'm going to do is to see if he's got my bike in there, and if he has, then I'm going to take it back, because it's mine. And it's him who's pinched it from me. Not the other way round.' But I couldn't help wishing that Johnny Merry was with me, because then I'd be feeling a bit braver if there was the two of us doing it together. We'd sort of egg each other on, wouldn't we.

I crept over to the window and listened, and couldn't hear any noise at all. So I plucked up all me courage and ever so carefully slid the window up. Me heart was thumping so hard it was like it was going to bust and me breath was panting.

I put me hands inside to feel if there was anything in the way and then ... Something bit onto me finger. And it didn't half hurt!

I skreeked out ever so loud and snatched me hands back, and there was a great big ferret hanging onto me finger. It was agony! I tried to shake it off, but it wouldn't let go, and I was skreeking and bawling, and then all along the street the lights went on, and in Fred Ferret's house as well, and him and all his neighbours come pouring out into the street roaring, 'Kill! Kill! Kill!'

At least, that's what it sounded like they was roaring.

I didn't half run, I'll tell you. And the ferret run with me, because it wouldn't let go of me finger.

They chased me for miles before I got away. But I couldn't get away from the ferret, and me finger was pouring with blood, and the pain was awful, and it didn't matter how much I shook me hand and pulled at the ferret it just wouldn't let go.

I daren't go home with the ferret, because me Mam would go mad if I did. Since our last cat died and Sid's rabbits all escaped and caused her all that trouble she won't have any animals in our house at all, you know.

So I thought I'd go and ask Mr Sambourn if he could help me.

He was brilliant! He just got hold of the ferret's neck and squeezed and it let go. Then he patted and stroked it until it was all nice and quiet. Then he washed me finger and put iodine on the holes the ferret's teeth had made, and bandaged it up.

After I'd give him the full story about me bike, he just smiled and shook his head.

'I fear Specs, that you have been out-generalled by Mr Frederick Ferret. It appears to me that he laid an ambush for you, and you walked right into it.'

He had a good look at the ferret then.

'This is a very fine animal, Specs. I shouldn't think that Frederick Ferret bargained on you taking it with you upon your departure. Wait here until I return.'

He put the ferret in a cardboard box and took it with him.

He come back about an hour later, and guess what? He had me bike with him.

After I'd said thanks, because I really was ever so grateful, he told me, 'Allow me to offer you some advice, my young friend. If in future you decide to go poaching from the wicked squire, then make sure you do not tread on the toes of the wicked poachers. They will resent your taking the game quite as much, if not more, than the wicked squire will. They regard it as their own property, you see.

'I would also advise that you let bygones

be bygones regarding the theft of your bicycle. Look upon all of this as a slice of excellent experience of life, Specs.'

So that's what I'm going to do.

Eighteen

I aren't half fed-up. Nobody is speaking to me in our house. I've been sent to Coventry, just like one of them Blacklegs. It's because of me Mam. She's forbid everybody to talk to me.

It's been like this ever since the copper come with the summons for me, and she found out about me being in trouble for poaching.

'You wicked, rotten, ungrateful, thievin' little bleeder,' she skreeked at me. 'You'se ruined my good name in this town! I shall never be able to hold me yed up again in decent, respectable company.'

She was skreeking all this at me out in the street, because the copper come while I was at work, you see, so me Mam was waiting for me outside the front door when I come back from work.

'You aren't never going to cross this doorstep again, you evil swine,' she was roaring. 'So bugger off and never darken my door again.'

All the neighbours was hanging out of their doors and windows listening to her, and I could feel meself going all red in the face when I heard them laughing.

'What's he done, Effie?' Doreen Merry shouted.

Of course, Doreen knew all along what I'd done, didn't she. But she was just stirring me Mam up for devilment.

Me Mam was that mad at me that she forgot she wasn't talking to Doreen, and she told her, 'He's destroyed the fair name of Kensal. He's brought disgrace on my home.'

Then me Mam remembered that her and Doreen had fell out and wasn't speaking. So she went straight into action. 'And it's all your bloody fault, Doreen Merry. That bloody whelp of a brother of yours has led this silly simple-minded bleeder into wicked ways.'

Well, I reckon that was a bit uncalled for, wasn't it. Calling me simple-minded like that. Do you know there's times that I don't believe that I am her son, you know.

Because Mams am expected to stick up for their kids, aren't they. And she never ever sticks up for me, and she never has done neither, not even when I aren't done nothing wrong and I'm getting blamed for something that I haven't done. If anybody ever says a bad word against me, she adds on another three of the same.

Doreen wasn't backwards about coming forwards, I'll tell you.

'Don't you go becalling my brother, Effie Kensal. That son of yours is the slyest little sod that God ever put breath into. He only acts stupid and daft, but underneath he's the Spawn of the Devil.'

Blimey! It's getting worse, aren't it. I wonder what they'll be calling me next?

Me Mam got all scornful then. 'O'course, it's all right for you, aren't it, Doreen Merry. Because you've never had a good name to lose, have you. You've always been Po' White Trash!'

'Po' White Trash.' I know where me Mam got that from. It's from that film, *Gone with the Wind*. She's seen it a hundred times, and she knows it by heart. She always says that if she hadn't had me she could have played the part of Scarlet O'Hara. She says that she was down town one day and that this Yank come driving along in a big white car. When he saw her he stopped the car and asked her if she could come to Hollywood with him and play the part of Scarlet O'Hara. But she told him no, because she couldn't leave her fatherless children by themselves. She says the Yank told her that she could bring our Virgy with her because Virgy was a pretty babby, but she couldn't bring me because I was too ugly, and if people found out that such a beautiful woman had such an ugly babby they'd think that there was something wrong with her. She says that the Yank begged her to put me into an orphanage and forget all about me, and then he'd make her a film star. But she still told him no.

She always finishes this story by skreeking at me, 'If it wasn't for you, you ugly, four-eyed bleeder, I'd have been a bleedin' film star now and living in the lap of luxury, and be married to Clark Gable. You've ruined my life, you have!'

To tell you the truth, I wish that she had put me in an orphanage. I might have been adopted by a nice kind-hearted woman then, mightn't I. And anyway, I don't know where she gets off keeping on telling me how ugly I am, she ought to take a good look at herself in the mirror sometime.

When she called Doreen Merry, 'Po' White Trash', all the neighbours cheered and clapped, and Mrs Masters shouted, 'Fifteen to love. Mrs Kensal leads. Miss Merry's service.'

But Doreen never skreeked back. She only grinned and tapped the side of her nose with her finger, and said all quiet and smug, 'We'll see who's "Po' White Trash" when we goes to court. We'll see who the Magistrates thinks are "Po' White Trash", won't we.'

Then she put her head back inside and pulled the window down.

Mrs Masters shouted to me, 'If your Mam chucks you out, Specs, you can come and stay with me.'

'He's going nowhere to stay.' Me Mam didn't like that at all. 'He stays with me. I aren't spent all my money on him all these years for him to bugger off now that he's working and earning. He's got to pay me back now for all that I'se sacrificed for him. Get in this house right this minute, Specs.'

When I went past her Mrs Masters

winked and whispered, 'I thought that 'ud get you back into your own home, Specs.'

I wasn't that pleased really, because I reckon I'd sooner live with Mrs Masters than with me Mam.

When I got into the house me Mam told everybody, 'No one is to speak to this wicked bleeder until I says that they can.'

Uncle Harold and Hilda looked upset, but they're both too scared of me Mam to argue the toss. And Sid and me Dad likes to see me in trouble with me Mam because it keeps her off their backs, so they never said a word about it. As for our Virgy ... Need I say more?

Nineteen

Well, I got good news, and bad news to tell you.

The good news is that me Mam is on my side, for once. And everybody in the house is speaking to me again.

The bad news is that Doreen Merry knew what she was talking about alright.

The Kensals really are 'Po' White Trash'.

Yeah! It's true! That's what the magistrate called us!

And another bit of bad news is that I messed up me chance to speak to Sophia. You know who she is, don't you. She's that beautiful dark-haired girl who I saw playing tennis with Aubrey Jones-Evans.

When me and Johnny Merry went to court this morning I had a bit of a shock because Doreen Merry wouldn't let Johnny come near me, not even to say Hiya. And me Mam was with me so we couldn't sneak off somewhere and say Hiya then. So me and Johnny just made a few secret signs to each other.

Another thing that shocked me as well was seeing Fred Ferret and Stargazer sitting on a bench in the passage outside the court room. Stargazer was in his beret with feathers on it and his kilt and wellies, but he had a rabbitskin jacket instead of his fox fur, and it didn't half stink bad, I'll tell you. He was having an argument with the ceiling and by the way he was shouting, the ceiling was winning.

An old copper with a lot of medal ribbons come out and told him to shut up, but Stargazer took no notice, and the copper come up to him and grabbed his shoulder. Next thing you know, the copper's face turned green, and he shouted, 'Gas! Gas! Gas!' and run outside and we didn't see him again.

Then a copper come to fetch me into the courtroom. When me Mam went to come with me he told her, 'You'll have to go into the public gallery, Missus.'

She started cussing and swearing under her breath, but he just said again, 'Public Gallery, Missus. But don't worry, you won't miss any of the show, because it's not really a gallery, it's just some benches in front of the magistrates and clerks' benches.'

I had another shock when I got inside and saw who the magistrates were.

Idris Jones-Evans and Doreen Merry's 'Fancy Man', old Albert Harper.

Me Mam started having a bit of a scuffle with some blokes and women on the front row because they wouldn't hutch-up and let her sit down.

Idris Jones-Evans glared daggers at her. 'Will that woman kindly sit down and be quiet. This is a Court of Law, not a low-life public house.'

She glared daggers back at him, and

plopped herself down between two old blokes and they glared daggers at her, but hutched-up.

And then I had the biggest shock of all, because when I looked at the people on the rows of benches I saw Sophia! She was wearing a white dress and her long black hair was hanging over her shoulders, and she looked ever so beautiful.

All of a sudden I remembered that film when Ronald Colman was on trial because he was pretending to be somebody else, and he said, 'It is a far, far greater thing that I do now, than I have ever done.' He did it because he was in love with that girl, didn't he.

I'll tell you, I didn't half wish that I was wearing a Foreign Legion uniform and looking all dashing and handsome like Ronald Colman, instead of wearing me old blue suit which is too short for me in the sleeves and legs and looking like I does, a proper prat.

I couldn't help but keep on squinting on the sly at Sophia, and once when I did she sort of smiled at me, and she lifted her hand like she was telling me hello and good luck and giving me the Victory sign.

O'course she might have been giving me the other V sign and telling me to sod off and stop looking at her. But it didn't seem like she was doing that. I hoped she wasn't anyway.

They told me I was charged with poaching and asked me if I was guilty or not, and I said I wasn't. Because I hadn't poached anything, had I. I know that I tried to, but I hadn't found any pheasants, had I.

Then they said they was going to call the prosecution witnesses.

First of all the gamekeeper come. Then the coppers. And then Fred Ferret. What an old Toe Rag he's turned out to be! And I always thought he was a sort of mate of mine.

He stood in the witness box pointing at me and going, 'Ahrrr Ahrrr Ahrrr Ahrrr.'

And Idris Jones-Evans kept on interrupting and saying, 'Can this witness please make himself intelligible to the Bench?'

And the clerk bloke kept bowing and scraping, 'Yes, your Worship. No, your Worship. Three bags full, your Worship.'

And the people started laughing, and Fred Ferret kept on going, 'Ahrrr Ahrrr Ahrrr Ahrrr.'

In the end they sent Fred Ferret out of the room because they couldn't understand anything he was saying. Good job as well, because it was all lies about how he'd seen me and Johnny Merry poaching pheasants lots of times, the lying Toe Rag!

Then they fetched Stargazer in.

When the copper tried to give him the Bible to swear the oath on, Stargazer didn't even try to take it. He just let the copper drop it on the floor every time, while he kept on talking to the ceiling. He was laughing and chuckling to himself.

'... Oh that's a good one. I haven't heard that one before. Where did you say that you heard it first? Oh, in Vienna, you say. Unfortunately I've never had the opportunity to visit Vienna but I have made a close study of the history of the Hapsburg Dynasty and the early economic history of the Austro-Hungarian Empire. I find the surveys of the Galician provinces' turnip production during the eighteenth century particularly interesting ...'

'Get him out of here! Get him out of here! Get him out of here!' Idris Jones-Evans was going mental, and all the people, even the coppers, were roaring with laughing.

Idris Jones-Evans saw me laughing, and he shouted all angry, 'I'm glad you find it funny, Kensal. But this will wipe the smile off your face. I find you guilty as charged and you will be fined one hundred pounds.'

Me Mam, nearly hit the roof. She shot up from the bench and shouted, 'You can't do that to my babby. He's told you that he never done nothing. So you can't find him guilty.'

'Sit down,' Idris Jones-Evans shouted at her.

'Don't you tell me to sit down, you bloody jumped-up Taffy pit-prop,' she told him. 'I can remember you when you kept your coal in the bath. And another thing, what was you doing in the war when my husband, this poor child's father, was away fighting for his King and Country? You was sitting back here at home lining your own pockets, and playing at being a bloody soldier in the bloody Home Guard, you bloody "Royal Standback".'

'How dare you call me a Taffy pit-prop, you "Po' White Trash",' he skreeked back at her, and then the two of them started fighting each other across the counter in front of his chair.

'Go for it, Girl!' one of the old blokes shouted, and then everybody else joined in egging her on. All the coppers come blowing their whistles and they had to drag me Mam and Idris Jones-Evans apart and take them both outside.

When I looked at Sophia she really smiled at me this time, and waved. I felt meself going all red in the face but it still felt ever so good and I was really happy. I didn't care what they did to me now.

But they didn't do anything.

There was a lot of whispering between the coppers and the clerks and old Albert Harper and in the end old Albert Harper said that in view of the unfortunate incident which had taken place during this trial I should be discharged on a technicality, and Johnny Merry was discharged as well. He never even had to come into the court room.

When I got outside I couldn't see me Mam anywhere but Doreen Merry was grinning all over her face. Albert Harper come out into the passage then and when he went past Doreen I saw him pinch her backside and wink at her, and she winked back and whispered, 'See you tonight, Albie, my old duck.'

I took it all in then. The reason why Doreen Merry wouldn't let Johnny come near me. It was because she'd already fixed it up with old Albert Harper, her Fancy Man, to get Johnny off. I reckon that if me Mam hadn't started fighting with Idris Jones-Evans then I'd have been sent to jail, or something, and Johnny Merry would have got away with it.

Do you know, I'm beginning to wonder if Johnny Merry is as good a mate of mine as he says he is. I mean to say, I wouldn't have let me Mam arrange to get me off and leave him to take all the blame by himself, would I.

Then me Mam come out of the police station, and she was grinning all over her face as well.

'Come on, Specs. I'm bringing you back from Coventry,' she told me all happily. 'Let's go home and have summat to ate. I put that bloody Taffy pit-prop in his place, didn't I. I been waiting for years for a chance to do that. And it's all thanks to you, Specs, that it's finally happened.'

I was that pleased to be released from Coventry that I just said, 'Yeah Mam, you really put that Taffy pit-prop in his place, didn't you,' and went back home with her.

Because I thought that if I didn't I'd only get her mad again, and she'd send me back to Coventry.

But what I really wanted to do then, was to stay near to Sophia. I mean to say, I might never get another chance to speak to her. And she'd really smiled at me, hadn't she. So I could have spoken to her, couldn't I. It could have been my big chance to get to know her, couldn't it.

I wonder why does life always seem to work out in the wrong way for me? Is it because that I really am like Doreen Merry says I am? Simple-minded?

Twenty

I had a bit of a fright last night, you know. But it was a great laugh, as well.

I've never been with a girl, you see. Not properly been with one, I mean. But Johnny Merry has, and he says it's great. And he's been saying for ages that he knows a girl named Tessa who would do it with me if I wanted. He says she does it all the time, because she likes doing it so much. So last night I told him that I'd go down with him to see this girl and ask her if she'd do it with me.

I was ever so nervous when we started off, but I was trying to hide that and be all cool and act like a Big City Slicker.

This girl lives down on the other side of the town, and down her road there's some Blackies from Jamaica come to live. You ought to see them, all pegtop trousers and wide-brimmed hats. A lot of the locals don't like the Blackies coming to live in our town, but I don't think like that because I think that the Blackies are only having an adventure when they come here, and I want to travel abroad and have adventures so that's the same for them as for me, isn't it. I reckon it's makes things more interesting when there's all different sorts of people living in one place. I mean, look at the Foreign Legion, there's all sorts there and that must be one of the most interesting places you can ever be in.

It's funny though how people act about the Blackies coming here. Mrs Masters, who's the nicest woman I've ever known in my life, can't stand them. But Doreen Merry thinks they're great. Sid hates them and keeps saying, 'They ought to all go back to the bloody jungle. They're the White Man's Burden, they am.'

I reckon that Sid hates everybody in the world, you know. He hates the Welsh and the Yanks and the Irish and the Scotch and the Germans and the Italians, the list just goes on and on.

But I don't know what me Dad thinks, because he's so crafty. He always agrees with whoever he's talking to at the time. If somebody says that they like Winston Churchill, me Dad tells them, 'That man is the greatest living Englishman. He's a wonderful man.'

But if somebody says they don't like Winston Churchill, me Dad tells them, 'He's a bloody warmonger. He ought to be put up against the wall and shot.'

I asked Mr Sambourn what he thought about the Blackies coming to live here, and he told me, 'Specs, in this world there are a few really good people, a few really bad people and a vast majority of people who are somewhere in between those two extremes, and race, colour and creed have no bearing on any of those categories. Respect all men, but fear no man, Specs, and treat all people as you would wish them to treat you. Remember that and you won't go far wrong.'

I think Mr Sambourn is very wise, you know. Even though some of the time I can't really understand what it is he's telling me. He's very deep, you know.

Of course me Mam says she hates the Blackies. But she only says that to aggravate Doreen Merry, because Doreen used to have Black Yanks as boyfriends when the war was on. There's one Blackie who walks down our street sometimes, and he's really good-looking, and whenever me Mam sees him she always smiles at him and tells him, 'Hello, lovely day, aren't it.'

Anyway, me and Johnny Merry were going down to see this girl, Tessa, her name is. Just as we get to the top of her road this woman comes walking towards us, and she's a real big hard-faced one, as well. She looks as if she could chew us both up and spit us out with no trouble.

'See that woman coming,' Johnny whispers. 'That's Bella, she's Tessa's mam.'

When she sees Johnny she stops dead, and if looks could kill, he'd have dropped dead on the spot.

'What's you doing down here, Johnny Merry?' She sort of spits the words at him. 'Because if youm going where I think youm going, I'll bleedin' well swing for you before you can take another step.'

You might think that this would be a shock to me, this woman doing this. But it wasn't. Ever since we was little kids people have been stopping dead in their tracks when they see Johnny Merry and threatening to swing for him.

Johnny did his Pretty Boy Romano, impression.

'Say, Lady, be cool, okay. Don't frazzle your hair. It's no big deal me coming onto your turf, okay.'

'If I catches you anywhere near my house I'll cut your balls off, you bloody big-yedded little bleeder. I'll give you, "Say Lady be cool okay".'

She was frothing at the mouth almost. But like I told you before, it's something I've lived with all me life.

It's strange how the older ones has always hated Johnny Merry, and yet all us younger ones thinks he's great.

'Okay, Honey Baby, it's cool. It's real cool!' Johnny is spreading his hands out like Pretty Boy Romano does in the film.

Just then a Blackie comes up the road behind her, and he's ever so big and tough-looking as well.

'Hey Bella, raasss bladclaat, somepin urnto zllowin,' he says to her. That's what it sounded like anyway.

I couldn't take it in, what he was saying, I mean. It sounded like Double-Dutch to me. But she understood alright. She must be clever, that's all I can say.

She smiled at the Blackie all gooey-eyed and they went off arm in arm. When he passed me and Johnny the Blackie glared at us, and his eyes went red. It's the truth. They went red! I wondered for a minute if he was a vampire. It put the fear of Christ up me, I'll tell you.

'Raasss bladclattt kinto hommo sallo Johnny Merry bladclaattt.'

'Yeah, you tell the little bleeder, Leroy,' Bella said.

'What did it mean?' I asked Johnny.

He just laughed. 'I'm buggered if I know, Specs. But I don't think that Blackie likes me very much.'

I was beginning to feel a bit nervous about going to see Tessa now. I mean, what if her mam and that Blackie come back while I was in the house with her?

But then I thought of how much I wanted to find out what it was like to do it with a girl, so I decided I'd risk it.

Bella's house looked ever so scruffy from the outside, all the windows was filthy and some of them were broke and had rags stuffed in the holes and the curtains was all torn. I know that me own house is scruffy as well, but at least me Mam keeps the windows and curtains clean. Then when Tessa opened the door there was a bad smell come from the inside. Tessa looked ever so scruffy as well, and her hair was all tangled and greasy and she had spots and she was fat.

To tell you the truth, I was beginning to think that I'd sooner not do it with her, but I couldn't back out of doing it because even though he's me mate, Johnny Merry would think I'm a real wimp if I backed out.

'Hiya, Baby.' Johnny was being Nicky Romano again. 'This is my Buddy, Specs. The one I told you about. He's come down to have a do with you.'

I could feel meself going all red in the face when he said that.

Tessa was chewing gum and smacking her lips ever so loud and she was staring at me like I was something the cat had brought in.

'He aren't very good-looking, is he,' she told Johnny. 'I don't like four-eyed blokes, you know.'

'He's a very nice bloke,' Johnny said. 'And he's better-looking than some of the other blokes you have a do with.'

'I suppose so,' she said. 'But if I has a do with him, then you've got to have a do with me first, because you know how much I likes you.'

Johnny looked all reluctant and I was hoping that he'd tell her no, and then we could leave without me doing it with her. But then he sighed very loud and said, 'Alright, I'll do it for Specs' sake.'

'Come on upstairs then.' She grabbed his hand and told me, 'You can wait in the front room, Four Eyes.'

To tell the truth I was wishing I'd never come.

Then as soon as I went into the front room I looked out of the window and saw Bella coming up to the front door with her boyfriend and a gang of other blackies. I went charging upstairs after Johnny and just got into the bedroom before the front door opened and they all came in.

Me and Johnny and Tessa was in the bedroom and we heard her mam shouting,

'Where am you, Tessa? Nevil's come to see you.'

'Bloody hell, me boyfriend's here.' Tessa wasn't half shocked. 'He gets ever so jealous of me having other blokes, you know. If he finds you two here him and his mates 'ull stick their knives into you.'

Then we heard footsteps coming upstairs and this bloke shouting, 'Where is you, Tessy honey?'

I got really scared then, I'll tell you, because me and Johnny wouldn't be able to fight the whole gang, would we. I could see us getting knives stuck into us all over. Me and Johnny run to the window, but we couldn't open it because it was nailed shut, so we couldn't jump down from it, could we.

'Quick,' Tessa told us. 'Get under the bed and hide.'

Just as we got under the bed the door opened and Nevil come in.

I was holding me breath and trying not to shiver in case he heard us.

Nevil sounded a bit mad as well. 'What you doing hiding up here, Tessy? Why didn't you answer me when I was acalling you? Has you got a man in here?'

Tessa didn't sound a bit scared of him though.

'Oh yes, that's right,' she shouted at him. 'I'se got blokes hid all over the bloody house, aren't I. In the bloody cupboards and under the bloody bed, and there's one there, hanging from the lightbulb.'

'Okay, okay,' he told her. 'There's no need to get vexed with me. It's only because I love you so much that I gets jealous.'

'Well I'm fed up with it.' Tessa was ever so snotty with him.

'I'm sorry, Tessy. I'm really sorry,' he kept on telling her, and then I could hear him kissing her, smacking his lips ever so loud.

They sat down on the side of the bed and she was still acting like she was mad at him.

'If you thinks that I'se got blokes in here why don't you look in the bloody cupboards and under the bloody bed?'

Blimey! I thought. I wish you wouldn't keep on telling him to do that.

And then he bent down to pull his shoelaces undone and he looked straight at me. His face was upside down and we was eyeball to eyeball, and his eyeballs bulged so much when he saw me that they was like two white footballs.

'Aggghhhhh!' He screamed ever so loud, and he jumped up and went running downstairs shouting, 'Raaassss Blooddclaaattt! Rasssss Rasss Rasss Blood-claaattt!'

There was a big hullaballoo downstairs, and I thought, bugger this for a game of soldiers. Me and Johnny shot out of that room and into the end room and we managed to get the window opened just as the gang of blackies come roaring in waving their knives in the air and screaming, 'Kill! Kill! Kill! Rasss Bloodclaattts! Kill! Kill! Kill!'

We dived through the window, and it didn't half hurt when I hit the ground, but there wasn't any time to stop and see what damage I'd done to meself.

We shot over the back yard fence and went haring away, and we could hear the blackies shouting, 'Kill!Kill!Kill! Raaassss Bloodclaaatts!' all the way up the road.

When we was safe we looked at each other and started roaring with laughing. But I'll tell you something, shall I ... I'm never ever going to go anywhere near that Tessa ever again ...

Twenty-One

Uncle Harold is going to be a monk!

He come home today and said, 'I've decided to renounce the world, and all its works. I'm going to be a monk. Most likely a Trappist monk, because I no longer even wish to speak. Instead I intend to spend the rest of my life in silent meditation.'

'What's brought this on?' Me Mam was really shocked. 'What the bloody hell does you want to be a monk for?'

'I know why he wants to be a monk.' Sid was nodding all know-all. 'It's because of that letter he's had from the Dole Office, aren't it. They're threatening to stop his dole aren't they. So he's got to find a job, hasn't he. And he'd sooner do anything rather than get a job, 'udden't he.'

'Shurrup!' me Mam shouted, and looking all worried she asked Uncle Harold, 'Why, Harold? Why does you want to be a monk? And what about Hilda? What's going to happen to Hilda if you goes into a bloody monastery?'

'Well, for all the good he is to her he might just as well be in a bloody monastery.' Sid was loving it. 'If Hilda's got any sense she'll pack his bags for him, and then go out and find herself a real man.'

Hilda's having to do a lot of overtime at work, you see, to earn some extra money. Because since Uncle Harold was sacked from Smiling Sam's he hasn't done any work at all, and he's only got a bit of Dole money coming in, so Hilda has to pay both their shares of the housekeeping money. Not that that's anything unusual for her.

'What does you think about it, Horace?' Sid asked me Dad then.

But me Dad was boxing crafty again. He was watching me Mam very close, and he could tell that she was getting upset about Uncle Harold going into a monastery. So he just kept quiet and bided his time.

Of course, I know what's going on, you know. I'm not as thick as they think I am. You see, me Mam is still trying to make up her mind about which one she's going to choose between Sid and me dad. And she's told both of them that when she makes her choice, then the loser has got to leave our house immediately and never darken its doors again. So they both keeps on trying to get into her good books.

'Hilda will understand that I need the peace and solitude of the Trappist life. She will be happy that I am going to tread salvation's path.' Uncle Harold was looking all soulful, and his eyes was shining joyfully.

At least I think they was shining joyfully, but it might have been the electric light reflecting off his glasses.

'Well, will you be able to come home for your holidays, Harold?' me Mam wanted to know.

'You haven't understood, have you, Effie, my dearest sister in the Lord.' Uncle Harold spoke ever so kind to her. 'When I enter the monastery I shall never ever step outside its blessed walls again. I shall never ever speak again. And I shall never ever see any of my family again. You must think of me as having gone to Heaven.'

'We can come and see you, can't we?' Me Mam acted like she couldn't believe what she was hearing. 'I mean, it 'ull be a nice day out for me and Virgy to come and see you and have a cup of tea and a look around the Monastery.'

Uncle Harold shook his head, and he was sort of sorrowful but still happy, if you know what I mean. But to tell you the truth, I don't really know what I mean meself.

'No, my dearest Sister, you will never see me in this garment of earthly flesh again. No one may enter the walls of the monastery except for my Blessed Brothers in Christ.'

'Ohhhhh, Harold!' me Mam wailed, all distressed.

'Your bleedin' blessed brothers?' Now it was Sid who was acting like he couldn't believe what he was hearing. 'You aren't got any brothers!'

Uncle Harold just smiled at him, but didn't say nothing, and Sid lost his rag a bit then.

'I'll tell you what, Mate. It aren't a bloody monastery you ought to be going to. It's a bloody Loony Bin. You've gone off your yed, you have.'

'You leave my Harold alone, you.' Me Mam went for Sid then. 'If you'd been nicer to him, he wouldn't have gone of his yed, would he. Because you've been so rotten to him all these years it's all your fault that he's gone bleedin' loony. I can't bear to think of him going away from me like this. What if he don't like it once he's in the bleedin' monastery, and them bleedin' monks won't let him out again?'

I'll tell you what, I've got to hand it to me Dad, he really is one of the craftiest blokes I've ever met in me life. He should have been a general, because he'd have won every battle he was in charge of. He saw an opportunity to really put one over on Sid, and he took it instantly.

'Now, now, let's all keep calm, shall we,' he said. 'Harold is most certainly not a Loony. In fact I consider him to be one of the most intelligent people I have ever met. But he's sensitive beyond the experience of any of us here in this room.'

He's using his posh voice now, and to tell you the truth he sounds like a real prat. But like Mr Sambourn keeps saying: 'When in Rome, do as the Romans'.

'Can I make a suggestion, Effie, darlint?' me Dad asked me Mam.

She just nodded, looking all wary and suspicious.

'Many thanks.' Me Dad nodded very graciously. 'Now, the problem as I see it is that Harold wants to withdraw from all earthly contacts, and lead a life of solitude and meditation. Is this right, Harold? Have I understood correctly?'

'Indeed you have, Horace.' Uncle Harold was so happy that somebody was on his side that he started to cry and his glasses steamed up.

'And am I right in saying, Effie, darlint, that you do not wish Harold to enter this monastery and cut himself off from all earthly contact?'

'Yes, Horace.' Me Mam was looking all tearful now. 'I'm worried in case he don't like it once he's in there, and then he finds out that the bleeders won't let him come home to me again.'

'Well now, I have the perfect solution.' Me Dad was looking ever so smug. 'Harold can experience the monastic life without going into the monastery. He can see if it'll suit him or no. What I propose is this: we construct a monastic cell for Harold somewhere upon this property. So then he can be a monk, and you, Effie darlint, would still have your beloved brother here at home with you.'

'Ohhhhh, Horace, youm a bleedin' genius!' Me Mam threw herself at me Dad and wrapped her arms around his neck.

Sid was glaring daggers at them, and was doing what he calls his 'Tiger' look. That's when he curls his top lip up to show his teeth like a snarling tiger does. Only he'd took his teeth out when he was eating his dinner because they was hurting him and he'd forgot to put them back in, so he only looked all gummy.

Me Dad was rocking his head and grinning all smug at Sid. Then he asked Uncle Harold, 'What say you, Harold?' 'What say you, Harold?'

What say you, Harold? Where did me Dad get that from? It's great, aren't it! What say you, Harold? I'll have to remember that one.

Uncle Harold was delighted.

'That's a wonderful idea, Horace. I'll go in search of a suitable site immediately.'

He went rushing out into the back yard, and we could hear him singing, 'Nearer my God to Thee ...' He come back almost straight away.

'I've found the ideal place. We can convert the rabbit hutches. We can make one into my cell, and the other into my own private chapel. It will be wonderful!'

'I'll draw the conversion plans up this

very night, Harold.' Me Dad was all happy now with me Mam still wrapping her arms about his neck.

But Sid was livid with jealousy. 'Excussssse me, Horasssss Kenssssal,' he hissed like a snake. 'I think you're forgetting summat. You're forgetting that them rabbit hutches belongs to me. And it's me who says what can be done with them. Not you!'

Me Mam slitted her eyes at Sid then, and I reckon he must have realised that he was getting very near to getting the boot from her, because as quick as a flash he changed from Mr Nasty to Mr Nice.

'Harold, it is an honour and a privilege and a pleasure to present you with my rabbit hutches. Do whatever you want with them. They are yours now.'

'Ohhhhh, Sidney!' Me Mam unwrapped herself from me Dad and run and wrapped herself around Sid. 'That's really nice of you, that is.'

Now it was Sid's turn to rock his head and smile all smug at me Dad.

'No sacrifice of my property is too much for me so long as that sacrifice gives you and your Harold a bit of pleasure, Effie, my love.'

Strewth! I'm feeling like I could be sick by now, watching the way this lot goes on. Do other families behave like this, I ask myself? I mean to say, I know that Terry Murtagh's dad, when he's at home, keeps coming in drunk and chasing his missus and kids with an axe, and I know that since Mr Polson got religion he holds a family prayer meeting in his back yard for Fatty Polson and his Mam twice a day and three times on a Sunday, and I know that Bokker Duggan's Gran keeps chucking bricks through the police station windows because she blames them for sending Bokker's dad to prison for thieving. But all what they does seems normal somehow. But what my family gets up to just don't seem normal somehow.

Uncle Harold is beaming now. What's that word that I read in the dictionary last week? Oh yeah, I remember. He looks ecstatic.

'I'll have the conversion plans made for you by a proper architect, Harold.' Sid is really pouring it on thick now. He thinks that he's got me Dad on the run alright. 'You need a proper English conversion doing. Not one of them bloody Australian conversions. All they'se ever converted in

Australia is to put tin roofs on their mud huts, and most of 'um are still living in bloody caves anyway.'

I was waiting for me Dad to go mental now, but he never. He never said a word back to Sid. He just smiled all sadly at Uncle Harold and told him, 'I'm sorry that I shan't be permitted by Sidney Tompkin to help you with the conversion, Harold. But I'm sure that Sidney Tompkin will do an excellent job of the conversion. And rest assured that I shall pray for its success. In fact, if you will all be kind enough to excuse me, I shall go to my room and begin praying immediately.'

I was watching Sid's face while me Dad was saying this, and I could see that he was starting to look a bit more doubtful the more me Dad went on. And by the time me Dad went in the front room to start praying, Sid's face was beginning to look more than doubtful. It was looking real miserable.

He'd lumbered himself with the job, hadn't he. And Sid is useless at everything, and he don't like hard work any more than me Uncle Harold likes hard work. And that's not at all.

Of course, the rabbit hutches brings back

painful memories for Sid, you know. He bought them and had them set up at the bottom of our back garden in the War. He was going to have a rabbit farm and breed rabbits and sell them for meat and skins. But all the rabbits escaped and they caused ructions down our street for ages. It was like a Civil War because the rabbits was eating all the neighbour's plants and digging tunnels all over the place, and the neighbours was blaming Sid for it and telling him that they'd swing for him, and the police used to keep coming and threatening to put Sid in prison if he didn't pay for all the damage that the rabbits was doing. It made him a nervous wreck, I'll tell you.

I had to go out then because I'd arranged to go and see Mr Sambourn for a chess game. He always beats me because I'm just a learner, but he says that I'm getting better all the time at it.

While we was in his house playing chess I told him about me Uncle Harold becoming a monk, and how he was going to convert the old rabbit hutches and live in them all by himself without ever speaking to anybody and spend all his time meditating. Mr Samborn didn't half laugh.

'From what you've told me of your Uncle Harold, Specs, I rather doubt that he will find a life of eremetic monasticism altogether to his liking. And if at some future date he enters a Trappist Monastery he will find it to be a very austere and physically taxing existence. The Trappists are expected to perform very hard manual labour and practise extreme frugality in diet. They also of course operate the silent system.

'All in all, Specs, it is not the type of existence which would appeal to me, or to many other men, in my opinion.'

'Yeah, Mr Sambourn, but me Uncle Harold aren't like other men. He's different.'

Mr Sambourn just laughed again and nodded his head.

'He is most certainly that, Specs. Most certainly. Your Uncle Harold is really quite unique.'

When I thought about what Mr Sambourn had said, I began to feel really proud of me Uncle Harold, you know. Because it's true, aren't it. He is unique. There's nobody else like me Uncle Harold in the whole of the world.

Twenty-Two

Do you reckon I'm weird because I don't like football? Because everybody else round our way loves it. All me mates, and Georgie Snood and the blokes at work, and Sid and me Dad, they all loves football. They talks about it for hours, but none of them actually plays it. What I mean is, that none of them are in a proper football team.

Now I don't mind having a bit of a kickabout, but I don't want to stand for hours watching other blokes do it.

And another thing that I can't understand is this business of being Football Supporters. Like Georgie Snood, for example. He loves Aston Villa. But he never goes up to Brummagem to watch them play. In fact I don't think that he's ever seen them play. But he reads the *Sporting Pink* every Saturday night to see how they got on, and if they've won he's happy all the week. Well, not happy exactly, but he aren't so miserable and sour as he is when they loses. He gets all upset if anybody says anything bad about the Villa, and he spends hours arguing about who should be in the team, and how the Villa should have won this match, and why they didn't win that match. But the only thing he knows about how they played in any match is what he reads in the *Sporting Pink.* And most Saturday all that the *Sporting Pink* says is whether the Villa won or lost, and there might be a couple or three sentences about how the goals was scored.

All the other blokes that he argues with are the same. They never goes to watch the teams that they supports, but they argues and fights about them all the time.

I can't take it in, you know. I really can't.

I asked Mr Sambourn what he thought, and he laughed and told me, 'Well, Specs, my father once remarked to me that Soccer is a Gentlemen's game played by hooligans, and Rugby is a hooligans' game played by Gentlemen. Personally I've no interest in either pursuit. Apart from that I have no further comment to make. Except for the observation that if thousands of men wish to spend their weekends chasing inflated bladders around a field, and if millions of other men who never see a game wish to argue about it, then who are we to say them nay ...'

Mr Sambourn comes out with some great stuff, don't he. I wish I could talk like him.

Anyway, I don't know why I'm going on about football, because what I wanted to tell you was about me Dad.

He's been chucked off the dole! Yeah, it's true! He went down the other day to sign on and to get his money, and the bloke behind the counter told him, 'There's nothing for you this week, Mr Kensal. And the manager wants to see you right away.'

Now I don't know what the manager said to him, because me Dad won't tell us. But another bloke I know was in the Dole Office when me Dad went into the manager's office, and he told me that me Dad was as white as a sheet when he come out of it.

When me Dad came home he was swearing and cussing about the Dole Office and the government and everything else in the world.

'Oh, give it a rest will you, Horace.' Me Mam got fed up with listening to him.

'What does it matter if they've stopped your dole money? You told me that your own money was coming through next week, didn't you. We'll all be rolling in clover then, won't we.'

That shut him up. I was looking at him very closely, and I could see that he got all wary when me Mam said about his money coming.

There's times I think that me Mam is dead thick, you know. I mean really stupid! Every week me dad tells her that the money is coming next week, and then he makes some excuse or other when it don't come, and tells her that it'll definitely come on the next week. And every week she swallows his old abdab.

To me it's as clear as the day that there's no money coming from Australia or anywhere else for me Dad. And no luggage neither. He's still wearing the clothes he come in, and it's starting to show, if you get what I mean. He's beginning to look like a walking rag and bone stall.

Sid is loving it. What he does now every day is to ask me Dad ever so sweetly, 'Any news about the vessel that is bringing your extensive wardrobe to Old England's shores, Horace, Old Bean?'

At first me Dad just used to ignore him, but then one day he made a fatal mistake. He got a bit irked and told Sid, 'Well, it's none of your bloody business, Sidney Tompkin, but I'll tell you anyway. The shipping company has telegraphed me to inform me that there was a typhoon in the Bay of Biscay which damaged the boat my luggage was on. So it all had to be transferred to another boat, but that boat has got to go to Hong Kong before it can come to England, so it could take some considerable time for my luggage to arrive.'

Sid never said a word. He just grinned fiendishly and now every time he sees me Dad he starts singing that song:

'I'd like to get you, on a slow boat to China ...'

I reckon everybody in the town knows now that me Dad is just bullshitting when he says he's got money coming. Everybody except me Mam. She still believes him. That's why I said I reckon she's dead thick at times. But she's never thick in other directions. She's on to me like a ton of bricks if I ever try to get away without paying me board and lodging. I have to cough up all of it every pay day or I'd be out on the street. But me Dad has never put a penny in the housekeeping ever since he come back. He lives here for nothing, and he lives on the fat of the land as well. Me Mam buys him all sorts of Fancies, but she never buys them for anybody else. Not even for our Virgy or Uncle Harold.

Mind you, thinking about it, perhaps me Mam aren't that thick about me Dad after all. Because it's not costing her anything to keep him, is it. All she's done is to cut down on the rations of the rest of us. I mean, I used to have two mutton chops for me Saturday dinner, but now she only gives me one. Me Dad has the other. And it's the same when I have some bacon. Now she only gives me one rasher, and she gives the other to me Dad. She does this to Uncle Harold as well, because she knows that he's got his head too far into the clouds to realise what's happening. She forgot one day, and she put two rashers of bacon on Uncle Harold's bacon butty, and he'd just took a bite when she skreeked, 'Stop, Harold! Stop chewing!' And she snatched the butty from him and opened it up and took out one of the pieces of bacon.

'That's for Horace,' she said. 'He always fancies a bit of bacon when he gets back from the pub.'

'That aren't all he fancies, is it,' Sid said, all snotty.

'No, but it's all he gets,' me Mam told him ever so haughty.

'It's all I gets as well though, aren't it.' Sid was really pathetic now.

Me Mam smiled, very superior. 'You'se just got to be patient, Sidney Tompkin. Until I makes me mind up which one of you I really wants.'

Sid put on his Humphrey Bogart look then. 'It aren't easy for a guy like me to be patient, Effie. I'm a guy of passion and hot blood. When there's a sweet doll like you in the next room, it's hard for a guy like me to control meself.'

Me Mam was really preening herself now. But like he always does, Sid has to go that bridge too far, don't he.

He give her a real smouldering look and whispered all husky-like, 'My hot blood 'ull probably drive me into coming into your room tonight, Effie.'

She went berserk!

'You try that on, you bleeder, and it'll be your hot blood all over the bleeding floor. I'll be taking the carving knife to bed with me, Sidney Tompkin, and if I feels that bloody snakey thing of yours coming anywhere near me in the night, I'll cut the bloody thing off.'

He went all grey-faced and sweaty.

'Now, now, Effie, calm down, my darling. Calm down, my dearest one.'

But me Mam was going full pelt now, just like a runaway train. 'You effin' bastard! I'll teach you to think you can make free with my body! Who the bleedin' Hell does you think you am, Sid Tompkin? I'll show you, you bleeder!'

I got me coat and went out, because although I don't like Sidney Tompkin very much, I didn't want to be a witness to his murder.

But it's me Dad I'm telling you about now, aren't it.

Well, after he'd come home from the Dole Office swearing and cussing, he was just starting to cool down a bit, when there came a knock on the door.

It was a bloke from the Labour Exchange.

When me Dad saw who it was he shouted, 'What does you want? I've seen enough of you already this morning to last me a lifetime. Just bugger off, unless you've come to tell me that I'm being let back on the Dole.'

I suppose I should have explained before. But the Dole Office and the Labour Exchange are both the same thing really. So that's why me Dad knew the bloke who'd come to the door. Because he was the same bloke that he had to see when he went to sign on for the Dole and collect his Dole money.

'I've got good news for you, Mr Kensal. But the Manager has sent me to bring you to him, because he wants to give you the good news himself in person,' the bloke tells me Dad now.

I could see the thoughts pounding around in me Dad's head because all the veins and arteries running up the side of his head was throbbing and jumping about.

'What sort of good news?' He wants to know.

But the Labour Exchange bloke only smiled and shook his head. 'I'm sorry, Mr Kensal, but it's more than my job's worth to tell you what the good news is. However, I can assure you that you will be delighted by it.'

Me Dad went with him then. And after about an hour there was another knock at the door, and who should it be but the bloke from the Labour Exchange again.

'The manager sends his compliments,' he says to me Mam 'and requests that you send transport of some type to remove your husband from the premises of the Labour Exchange.'

Me Mam can't take it in. 'What does you mean? What does he need transport for? What sort of transport, anyway? And where does your bloody manager think that I'm going to get transport from?'

Every sentence she was saying, her voice was going higher and louder, because she was working herself up to go mental.

I reckon that the bloke from the Labour Exchange could see what was coming, because he told her ever so quick, 'Your husband has suffered some sort of seizure, Mrs Kensal. He's laying on the floor of the manager's office screaming and groaning and frothing at the mouth. And the manager wants him moving because the Area Manager is coming in later today to discuss various matters.'

'What happened?' Me Mam was a bit deflected by the news, and she forgot that she was busy working herself up to go mental, and was all calm again.

'Well, the manager informed Mr Kensal that he had found him a job which he must start immediately, because if he refused it, the manager would ensure that he would be prosecuted for making a false statement in order to claim the dole. The manager would also ensure that Mr Kensal could never claim any sort of dole or national assistance ever again.'

'What sort of job is it?' me Mam asked him.

'A permanent position in the Council Sanitary Department,' the bloke told her. 'Initially Mr Kensal will be working on the Refuse Collection, but after he has been with the Council for six months he then becomes qualified to apply for any vacancies that occur in the Public Toilet Cleansing Division.'

When he heard this, Sid roared with laughing. 'It's true, aren't it, what they says.'

'And what does they say?' Me Mam was glaring at him now, but Sid, for once, didn't seem bothered.

'Well, they says that in this life every man eventually reaches the position for which he is most suited, and the level he deserves. It's proved right in Horace Kensal's case, aren't it.'

I was expecting to see the roof cave in on him now, but me Mam just looked all thoughtful.

'What does you mean about me husband making a false statement to draw the Dole?' she asked the Labour Exchange bloke.

'I'm sorry, Mrs Kensal, I am not allowed to divulge that information.' He shouted this over his shoulder as he was scarpering. 'And please send the transport for your husband just as quick as you possibly can.'

'Specs,' me Mam told me. 'Take your Uncle Harold with you and borrow the handcart from the Co-op yard. Fetch your dad straight back here. There's summat I wants to ask him about.'

I had to go down the back garden to find Uncle Harold. He was sitting in the rabbit hutch with his head bent down between his knees. He has to sit with his head bent down because the rabbit hutch has got a low roof, you see, and me Uncle Harold is a tall bloke. Only it's not called the rabbit hutch anymore. Uncle Harold says that it's his 'Hermitage', and that's what we all have to call it now.

He doesn't wear any proper clothes anymore neither. He got some sacks and Hilda made them into a hooded robe for him to wear. And he wears sandals all the time now, as well, but he keeps his socks on because he says his feet gets too cold if he don't. He's growing a beard, as well, but it's only a few straggly hairs because Uncle Harold aren't what you'd call a hairy bloke.

Sid said to me one day, 'Your Uncle Harold aren't man enough to grow a proper beard, not like me. My beard 'ud be a foot long in no time if I left off shaving. You should have seen the beard I grew when I went on that Antartic Expedition just before the war. The Eskimos used to call me, "Akka Makka Takka", that means, "The White Giant with Mighty Beard".'

I told you what a bullshitter he is, didn't I.

Me Mam heard him saying this, and she told him, 'The nearest you've ever been to the bloody Antartic is eating an ice cream.'

Sid looked very fierce then. 'That's all

you knows, Effie Kensal. I aren't allowed to tell anybody about that expedition because it comes under the Official Secrets Act. But some day the full story 'ull be told and then I'll receive my reward.'

'When did you go on this expedition then?' Me Mam wasn't going to let him off the hook this time.

'Before I knew you,' he told her.

'Well, why aren't you ever mentioned it before? You tells enough stories about every other bloody thing youm supposed to have done.' She can be real merciless me Mam can, you know.

While I was listening to them I remembered a book I'd got from the library which was all about Scott of the Antartic. In the book it said that there wasn't any Eskimos living in the Antartic, there wasn't any people there at all. Nobody lived there except the penguins and seals and whales and that.

I was just about to go and fetch the book so that I could make Sid own up that he was bullshitting. But all of a sudden I changed me mind. Because to tell you the truth I was starting to feel a bit sorry for Sid. Because ever since me Dad's come back he's really been put in the shade. Me Dad is always telling me Mam and Virgy stories about when he was a 'White Hunter' in Australia and all the safaris he's gone on, and all the lions and tigers and crocodiles he's shot.

Now I know for a fact that there aren't any wild tigers and lions in Australia and I told me Mam that. But she told me to mind me own business, and said that I didn't know anything about Australia because I'd never been there. And that me Dad had spent such a long time there that he knew everything there was to know about Australia, and if he said there was lions and tigers there, then there was lions and tigers there. She said that me Dad 'ud never dream of telling lies. He wasn't like that Sidney Tompkin who bullshitted all the time.

Now there's a turn up for the book! Before me Dad come back if I ever said to me Mam that I thought Sid was bullshitting about the things he said he'd done, she used to go mental at me and call me all the names under the sun, and tell me that Sid never ever told any lies.

When I told Mr Sambourn about how things had changed for Sid in our house, he just smiled and said, 'Behold, how are the mighty fallen.'

Anyway, I went down the back garden to fetch Uncle Harold, and he was sitting in his Hermitage. He goes there nearly every day, but he still lives in the house.

When he started being a Hermit he said he was going to take vows of poverty, chastity, solitude and silence.

'No need to take a vow of poverty, Harold,' me Mam told him. 'You're already living in that, like the rest of us in this house. And according to Hilda, you've got no need to take a vow of chastity neither. She reckons she aren't had a bit of the other for so long that she's forgot what it feels like. No, you just take them vows of solitude and silence, my lad. That'll do you to be going on with for now.'

So that's what he did. But the trouble was that because he wasn't speaking to anybody he couldn't go and buy himself a bag of chips when he got hungry, or tell Hilda what he'd like for his tea. So after a bit he thought it would be best if he didn't take the vow of silence after all.

Then he only spent the first day and night in solitude. He didn't spend the full night neither. Because Uncle Harold is frightened of the dark, you see, so when it got all dark and cold down the garden he nearly had one of his nervous breakdowns and he come running back into the house.

So what he's decided now is that he'll practise the vows of silence and solitude for a half hour each day when he goes and sits in his hermitage. He says that when he gets better at doing them, he might try and make it an hour or even longer.

'Come on, Uncle Harold,' I told him. 'You and me have got to borrow the Co-op's handcart and go and fetch me Dad from the Labour Exchange.'

'We have to fetch Brother Horace from the Labour Exchange? Whatever is he doing there? It's not the place where I would expect Brother Horace to spend his leisure hours.'

That's something I forgot to tell you before, but since Uncle Harold's become a hermit he calls all the blokes 'Brother' and all the women 'Sister'. Except for and me Mam, and Virgy. He even calls Hilda, Sister Hilda, and she gets all shirty every time he does it.

'Am you forgetting that me and you has had a passionate love affair, Harold?' she keeps on skreeking. 'It's a bit bleedin' late to make me be your bleedin' sister now, aren't it.'

Anyway, he come crawling out from the rabbit hutch, groaning and moaning because it always makes him very stiff to sit hunched up in it like he has to.

'Just a moment, Specs,' he said. 'I must fetch my Cross.'

Uncle Harold's cross is a great big wooden cross that he's made. It's ever so tall and wide and to carry it he's had to get one of them belt and pouch things that the soldiers carry their big flags in.

'It's no good bringing your cross with you,' I tell him. 'How are you going to help me push the handcart if you've got both hands on your cross?'

'Your father can hold the cross while we push him,' he said.

Well, he gets the cross and we go down the Front Hill to get to the Co-op yard where the handcart is.

Of course Uncle Harold attracts a lot of attention walking along in his hooded robe and sandals and carrying that big cross.

'Look out, here comes Jesus!' one bloke shouts and all the people who can see Uncle Harold start roaring with laughing, and shouting:

'Where's your donkey, Jesus?'

'I hope you aren't going to be hanging about on that bloody cross all day.'

'Who's that bloke in the specs you got with you, Jesus, is he one of the Apostles?'

Then some young kids start marching behind us singing, 'Glory, Glory Hallelujah. Glory, Glory Hallelujah.'

It's a funny thing though, but I never get bothered if people take the mickey out of me when I'm with Uncle Harold. What I think is, that if you can't take the heat, then don't go into the kitchen.

To be honest, for the way he goes on, and the things he gets up to, Uncle Harold asks for everything he gets in the way of mickey-taking, don't he. But what I like about him is that he doesn't give a bugger what anybody thinks of him. He couldn't care less. He don't even seem to know that people are laughing at him.

Mr Sambourn says that Uncle Harold is 'on the world, but not of it'.

I had to get Mr Sambourn to explain what he meant when he said that.

Then he said that Uncle Harold is insulated from the world around him by his own personal cocoon of innocence, and that he exists in a world inhabited by only one person, namely himself.

'But he lives with us, and he talks to a lot of people, and he used to sleep with Hilda. So how can he be living in a world inhabited only by himself?' I said.

'I don't mean live physically by himself, Specs,' Mr Sambourn told me. 'I mean that mentally he is the only inhabitant of his world, and a very wondrous world it is too.'

Well, when I was pushing that handcart up to the Labour Exchange I couldn't help but wish that Uncle Harold 'ud come out from his own world long enough to give me a hand with the pushing. The Co-op handcart is one of them old ones with massive big iron wheels and it aren't half heavy to push, I'll tell you.

Just as we got to the Labour Exchange me Dad come out of the big double door in the front of it. He wasn't walking though. He was laying all stiff on the ground and two of the blokes from the Labour Exchange, one old and one young, was rolling him over and over out onto the pavement.

'Hey, that's my Dad you're man-handling!' I shouted. 'What's the matter with him?'

'Bugger all!' The old bloke was really old and feeble and he was sweating and gasping for breath. 'He says he's making a protest against the inhuman treatment we've given him here.'

Then the young bloke noticed Uncle Harold and he did a double take and told me, 'Your Dad aren't near to death, you know. You didn't need to bring that bloody monk with you to give him the Last Rites.'

'He's not a monk. He's me Uncle Harold,' I said.

'Harold who?' The old bloke was staring real close at Uncle Harold, as though he thought he might know him.

'Harold Smith,' I told him.

'Harold Smith,' he said. 'Is that the same Harold Smith who used to help Smiling Sam the Undertaker to nail down the 'Stiff 'Uns'?'

'I am he, Brother,' Uncle Harold said all grandly. 'And may I inform you that my position with Smiling Sam entailed rather more than merely helping him to nail down the "Stiff 'Uns", as you so crudely put it. I was in fact Smiling Sam's Director of Burial Music and Ceremony.'

'Oh, were you indeed,' the old bloke said all sarcastic. 'Well forgive me, Mr Director of Burial Music and Ceremony, for failing to address you with due humility. Might I respectfully enquire what profession you are currently practising?'

'Certainly you may ask, Brother.' Uncle Harold didn't notice that the old bloke was being all sarky, and he was beaming at him. 'I have become a Hermit.'

'Have you now.' The old bloke acted all impressed. 'Well, isn't that wonderful, Charlie,' he said to the young bloke. 'Mr Harold Smith, late Director of Burial Music and Ceremony, has now become a hermit.'

'Well, well, well.' The young bloke acted all impressed as well. 'And might I respectfully enquire if being a hermit is a full-time occupation, Mr Smith?'

'It most certainly is, Brother.' Uncle Harold went a bit solemn then. 'And it is a most taxing occupation as well. I have to exert absolutely all of my mental and physical energies in order to make a success of it.'

'I'm sure you do,' the bloke said, then pretended to look puzzled. 'But what I can't understand, Mr Smith, is why you haven't notified this office of your new occupation?'

Uncle Harold looked really puzzled. And he wasn't pretending neither.

'Why should I do that?'

The old bloke come in then. 'Because, Mr Smith, you have been claiming unemployment benefit from this office ever since you left the employment of Smiling Sam. In simple, easy to understand terms, Mr Smith, you've been drawing the dole under false pretences.'

'Oh, God help me!' Uncle Harold looked all shocked and dismayed.

'I hardly think that God's intervention is required at this point in time, Mr Smith. However, perhaps at some later date you may indeed find it to be necessary to call upon His services. Anyways, as of this minute you are no longer entitled to draw any dole money. And in fact we shall be seeking repayment of the money you have defrauded us out of. You'll be lucky if you don't get sent to prison.'

'Oh my God!' Uncle Harold's glasses was starting to steam up, like they always does when he gets upset. 'It's all a terrible mistake.'

'It certainly is a very bad mistake from your point of view, Mr Smith.' The old bloke was looking really smug.

Another bloke came walking down the road then.

It was Idris Jones-Evans. He's been elected onto the Council now, you know, and he thinks he's the town's Emperor. When anybody speaks to him now he expects them to call him Mr Councillor Jones-Evans. Just like in the war when he was a captain in the Home Guards he made all us kids and everybody else call him Captain Jones-Evans.

When the two Labour Exchange blokes saw him coming they didn't half pull their faces about.

'Oh Jesus!' the old bloke muttered under his breath. 'I could have done without seeing this bloody fart come blowing up. You know what he's going to have a go about, don't you. Where are all the bloody new dustmen we promised him? Why haven't we recruited enough of them? He'll be bringing this matter up at the next Council Committee meeting and our heads 'ull be for the chop.'

'Eff him!' The younger bloke swore summat cruel. 'The way I feels at this minute I couldn't care less if he does get us both the sack.'

'Now hold on a minute, Charlie.' The old bloke looked scared to death. 'It might be alright for you to get the sack because youm still young enough to find another job. But I'se got my pension to think of. I'll lose it if I gets the sack from here. What are we going to do, Charlie? What are we going to do? We need more dustmen! And we need them now!'

The young bloke looked at me all speculative, and I told him quick, 'I works on the Gas, mate, so you can keep your beady eyes off me.'

Then the young bloke smiled at Uncle Harold, and asked him very silky, 'Tell me, Mr Smith, tell me again what it is you do?'

'I'm a hermit.' Uncle Harold was wiping his glasses on his robe, but because the sacks was all old and greasy he just kept on making his glasses greasier and dirtier and harder to see through, so when he put his glasses back on he was nearly blind, and he had to keep on taking them off and wiping them again. Only he didn't seem to catch on to what he was doing. I expect that was because he was so upset at the thought of having to go to prison.

'Not any more you're not, Mr Smith. From this moment on you are now a Dustman in the employment of the Urban Council.'

'What?' Uncle Harold dropped his glasses he was so shocked.

'You heard me, Mr Smith. The choice is simple. You either accept the position I'm offering you, or we have you prosecuted for drawing the Dole under False Pretences. I don't think prison would suit you at all, Mr Smith.'

Uncle Harold was a bit sharp for once though, and he come back straight away.

'On the contrary, Brother, I think that prison would suit me admirably. I should be in a cell, should I not? In solitary confinement on bread and water. A perfect place for a hermit like myself to live, I should say. Shouldn't you?'

The bloke just grinned all superior and shook his head ever so slow from side to side.

'Oh no, Mr Smith. You have to do something very wicked to get put into solitary on bread and water these days. And you aren't a wicked man, are you. So you'll be living in a cell with two other blokes, and you'll be eating three square meals a day. Oh, and you won't have any time for meditation, because you'll be sewing mailbags all the hours that God sends. And I don't think that you'll enjoy that job very much, will you? Especially since you'll be doing it for only a couple of shillings a week.

'Now, on the dustcarts you'll be earning a proper wage, plus whatever valuables you may find amongst the rubbish. I am given to understand that there are constantly being discovered all sorts of treasures, and many of our dustmen have been enabled to retire while still comparatively young and enjoy a very comfortable old age because they have discovered so many treasures.

'It's a golden opportunity for you, Mr Smith. I'm sure that there'll be no objection to you wearing your hermit's robes and taking your lovely big cross along with you. You can tie it onto the dustcart, and treat every day as a "Pilgrimage of Grace", can't you.'

Pilgrimage of Grace! Where did he get that one from, I wonder? It was a stroke of genius, you know, because I saw me Uncle Harold's face suddenly light up, and he kept on muttering, 'Pilgrimage of Grace. Pilgrimage of Grace. Pilgrimage of Grace.'

Idris Jones-Evans come up to us then, and the Labour Exchange blokes started sucking and crawling up to him, just like Georgie Snood does to the Gaffer.

'Yes, Mr Councillor Jones-Evans. No, Mr Councillor Jones-Evans. Three bags full, Mr Councillor Jones-Evans.'

'We've recruited the new dustmen, Sir. Fine chaps they are as well. Eager to get to grips with the rubbish. Thank you very much, Mr Councillor Jones-Evans.'

Idris Jones-Evans stood there like Lord Muck, and do you know he was too stuck-up even to give us a glance. But I knew that he knew us, because I'd seen him having a sly look at us when he was coming up the street. I don't know what he thinks he is exactly. But three like him wouldn't fill one of John Wayne's trouser legs, that's for sure.

Now me Dad was still laying as stiff as a board on the pavement outside the double doors, but he'd been listening very close to what was going on.

I reckon he could see a chance to finish off Sidney Tompkin for good and all with me Mam.

I reckon he was thinking that this was his chance to get to be real good friends with Uncle Harold, and if he was real good friends with Uncle Harold, then it meant that me Mam would like him more and more, wouldn't she. Because Uncle Harold always has been her all-time favourite above anybody else in the world. Even above our Virgy, and definitely above me. In fact I reckon I'm her least favourite person in the world, the way she keeps on having goes at me all the time. Mind you, she'll be sorry about how bad she's been to me when I'm marching off to Fort Zinderneuf to get killed by the Tuaregs.

Anyway, like I was saying, me Dad jumped up from the pavement and he told Uncle Harold, 'Here, Cobber, let me clean your glasses for you. We got to be looking at our best when we goes on our "Pilgrimage of Grace", aren't we.'

Uncle Harold was really moved. His eyes all filled up with tears and his voice was trembling. 'Do you really mean it, Brother Horace? Will you really accompany me on my Pilgrimage of Grace?'

'Too true, Blue,' me Dad told him. 'You and me will follow the Cross together, no matter what part of the town it takes us into. Shoulder to shoulder we'll march together in the Name of the Lord.'

'Oh Brother Horace, God Bless you and keep you!'

'Right then, Mr Kensal and you, Mr Smith,' the old bloke told them. 'Report to the Council Dust Yard tomorrow morning at seven o'clock sharp. And I'd advise you to wear some wellies, because those sandals you've got on will never keep the wet and mud out, Mr Smith.'

'Wet and mud!' Uncle Harold gasped, and then he had a little nervous breakdown, so we had to put him on the handcart and wheel him back home.

At least, I wheeled him back home. Me Dad disappeared into a pub before we'd got to the end of the street.

Twenty-Three

O 'course I got the blame, didn't I. For Uncle Harold having to go to work on the dustcarts, I mean.

'What a come down! What a show up!' me Mam was ranting and raving. 'And it's all your bloody fault, Specs. Our Harold is too refined to work on a bloody dustcart with all them roughs and scruffs. If you hadn't dragged him down to the Labour Exchange with you, then they'd never have found out about him and he'd still be a bloody monk. You've turned this family into the laughing stock of the town.'

I'll tell you what really upset her, shall I. It was when she went to do some shopping down town and the dustcart come past her with me Dad and Uncle Harold hanging on the back platform with half a dozen Pakis.

Me Dad had his big hat on with all the corks dangling from it, and Uncle Harold was wearing his robe and hood, and the Pakis was all wrapped in old scarfs and blankets and shivering blue with the cold.

Some of the neighbours saw them as well, and turned their noses up about it, because the dustmen are supposed to be beneath the factory workers. I can't see how that can be meself. We're all the same, aren't we. None of us has got two ha'pennies to rub together come Monday morning, has we. So I reckon that we're all in the same boat.

Did I tell you about the Pakis coming to live in the town? When they first come they was all wearing turbans and there was some women with them in saris. They looked ever so romantic and exotic.

I got that word exotic from Mr Sambourn.

I wanted to talk to the Pakis and ask them all about the North West Frontier, because I've been reading some books about it, but when I tried to talk to them none of them could understand me, and I couldn't understand them neither, so it was all a bit of a disappointment. And then, after a couple of days the weather got a bit chilly and they all started wearing big thick coats and scarfs round their earholes and they didn't look romantic or exotic anymore. Just cold and ordinary-looking like the rest of us, only instead of their faces turning all red with the cold, they turned blue.

Anyway, when Uncle Harold and me Dad started work on the dustcart some of the Pakis was working on it as well. Uncle Harold was thrilled about that. He likes anything new and different. But me Dad was really sour, and he come back home moaning and whinging.

'It aren't right, you know. I'm a Bwana and I shouldn't be having to do the same work as them coolies. I should be telling them what to do, not them telling me. And I should be riding in the cab of the cart with the driver, not that bloody Abdullah.'

That's what was really upsetting him, you see. Because the Foreman of the dustcart who sits with the driver in the cab is a Paki named Abdullah. He's the only one of them who can speak a bit of English, and he's tall and fierce-looking with a big moustache and a hooked nose like an eagle.

Me Dad's scared to death of him, because the first day on the job me Dad swore at him, and Abdullah pulled out this big curved knife and told me Dad, 'I swear by Allah and the Prophet that if you say one more vile word I shall send you to Shaitan.'

Me Dad nearly fainted, he was that scared.

'Shaitan' is the Paki name for the Devil, you know. Mr Sambourn told me that. And he told me that Allah is their name for God, and that Mahomet is their chief Prophet.

'That bloody Abdullah is a savage!' me Dad keeps on telling us now. 'A bloodthirsty savage. I takes me life in me hands every time I gets on that bloody dustcart. That bloody Abdullah 'ud knife a man as soon as look at him.'

But me Uncle Harold won't say a word against Abdullah. And I know that you'll find this very hard to believe, but me Uncle Harold loves working on the dustcart with the Pakis. He reckons that he might become a Moslem next year. He says that if he makes a pilgrimage to Mecca, that's a Holy City in the desert, then he'll be able to wear a green turban and a green gown, and he'll be able to dye his hair red, if he wants to.

'So much more attractive than the dull colours favoured by the Christian Brethren,

Specs,' he keeps on telling me. 'And just think how fiery and flamboyant red hair can be. It makes the tonsure pale into insignificance by comparison.'

Sid takes the mickey out of him though.

'I know what you wants, Harold You wants to have a lot of wives like them Pakis does, don't you. You sexy devil, you.'

Me Dad says that Uncle Harold is turning out to be really fly, and that he's only buttering up to the Pakis to get out of doing any work.

I reckon that Uncle Harold is boxing clever, you know. Because a bloke who works on the Council told me the other day that because Uncle Harold wears his robe and sandals all the time the Pakis thinks he's some sort of a Holy Man, and because of this Abdullah makes the rest of the Pakis do Uncle Harold's work for him.

I asked Mr Sambourn what he thought about that story, and he pondered for a bit, then told me, 'While not wishing to cause you any offence, Specs, or to cast any aspersions upon your Uncle's character, I have to point out that among Moslems there exists a popular belief that the mentally afflicted have been touched by the hand of Allah, and as such are under His special protection. Perhaps that might have some bearing upon Uncle Harold's present status among the Moslem dustmen.'

Well, I had to tell Mr Sambourn then that I'd known Uncle Harold was a bit Doolally Tap for years.

But I wants to tell you about something else that's ever so exciting.

I'm right in the middle of a great mystery! Yeah! Really! I'm right in the middle of it.

It all started a couple of weeks ago when me and Georgie Snood had to go and fit a new gas cooker at Mrs Splies' house down the bottom end of our street. Mrs Splies is a nice woman, but her husband, Old Splies, is a horrible bugger. Everybody calls him the 'Hairpin' because he's got something wrong with his spine and he's bent right over so that when he stands up his head nearly touches the ground.

Georgie Snood knows the Splieses and when he was give the job he got all nosy. Mind you, that's nothing new. He likes to know everybody's business. He's as bad as Clara the Clarion is. She lives at the top of our row, and me Mam reckons that she's the best newspaper in the world. Me Mam says that there aren't a thing that happens in the town that Clara the Clarion don't come to know about and broadcast for the world to hear. But I reckon that Georgie Snood is just as bad as Clara the Clarion for being nosy and spreading gossip about. It's interesting to listen to though, aren't it. Gossip, I mean. So long as it's not about yourself.

'What cooker have they bought?' Georgie Snood asked Herbert Taylor, the Stores Manager.

'A Trenton De Lux.' Herbert Taylor pulled a face. 'It's a bloody big cooker for just the two of 'um to use, aren't it. You could roast a bloody ostrich in the oven.'

'Ahh, it is big, aren't it.' Georgie Snood was nodding all thoughtful. Then he went to the hatch and called through to the office girls who work in the office on the other side of the hatch. 'This Trenton de Lux cooker for Splies. Whose name's on the invoice?'

'Mrs Mary Splies,' they told him.

'Is it now.' Georgie Snood was nodding his head like a yoyo. 'Is it now. Well, what about that then. It's her who's bought the cooker, not him. It's her. Well, what about that then.'

'Well, what about that then?' I asked him.

He just sneered at me then, and tapped his head. 'What's in here is for me to know, and you not to know.'

I can't take this in, you know. Why Georgie Snood is acting like this, I mean. What does it matter what size of cooker Mrs Splies buys? It's her business, aren't it.

We had to help load the cooker onto the van because it's so big one bloke can't handle it on his own. While we'em loading it Georgie Snood keeps saying to Benny the van driver, 'By Christ, you could roast a bloke in this bloody oven and still have room for the spuds, couldn't you.'

Benny is a massive tall ginger-headed Scotchman from Glasgow, and he talks ever so fast, so I can never tell what he's saying. Every time Georgie Snood says that to him, Benny goes, 'Harraaa Karraaa Barrrraaa Taarrrraaaa, Jimmy,' and laughs.

So me and Georgie Snood laughs every time as well, because if you don't laugh when Benny laughs he gets all red faced and bulgy-eyed like he's going mad and everybody's a bit scared of him when he gets like that, so to keep him happy everybody always laughs when he does.

When me and Georgie Snood gets to Mrs Splies house Benny is waiting for us and Clara the Clarion is there as well, talking to Benny. She can understand everything he says, you know. She's the only person in the whole of the town who can understand him.

Benny's wife is Irish, and she can't understand a word he says. I was talking to her one day and she told me, 'If I could understand what Benny was saying to me, I'm sure he'd drive me to distraction with his ould blether. Thanks be to God for His blessed mercy, that He's made me not able to understand nothing.'

We unloaded the stove and Benny drove off, and then Clara the Clarion whispered to us, 'I reckon we'll be seeing a funeral in this street in a few days.'

Georgie Snood nodded all wisely and whispered back, 'I reckon youm right there, Missus.'

I can't take this in. Why are they whispering about funerals? And whose funeral is it going to be? Because nobody's died in our street for ages, and I don't know of anybody who's dying.

Clara the Clarion was measuring the new cooker with her hands. 'There's ample room for him in this oven, aren't there,' she whispered to Georgie Snood, and he smiled ever so sly.

'Room for him and two others like him,' he whispered back.

All of a sudden I caught on then, and I knew what they was on about.

You see, Old Splies gets drunk a lot, and then he's ever so nasty to Mrs Splies and he hits her with his walking stick, so she don't like him very much at all. And another thing he keeps on doing is threatening to put his head in the gas oven and end it all. He's done it stacks of times, you know. He turns on the gas and then tries to put his head in the oven. But because he's so bent over his feet keeps getting in the way and he can't get his head inside.

Everybody reckons that he only does it for badness and to upset his missus and the neighbours. The neighbours gets upset because he fills the house with gas, and if somebody was to strike a match outside the house it would blow up and take half the street with it. His missus gets upset because every time he does it she has to be fetched from the shop where she works, and all the neighbours has a go at her for what Old Splies has done because they'm so scared that he'll blow them all up, and it's not her fault, is it. I reckon it's not fair to blame her for what he does.

But now she's bought this new gas cooker Old Splies will be able to roll his whole body into the oven, won't he. That's got to be the reason that she's bought it!

Blimey! She's crafty, aren't she!

Old Splies come and opened the front door then. It's ever so strange to see him talking to people, you know. Because he can't put his head far enough back to look up at you, so he has to stand sideways and turn his head up that way to look at you.

When he saw Clara the Clarion he got ever so nasty.

'What does you want, RentaGob? Go on, bugger off up to your own end of the street before I gives you a smack in the chops.'

'Phoo!' she went. She's not scared of nobody, Clara's not. 'You and whose army, Hairpin? I'm not your poor missus. You don't frit me, you old fart!'

'We've brought your new gas cooker, Mr Splies,' Georgie Snood smarmed. 'I'll have it fixed for you in two shakes of a donkey's tail, Sir.'

Old Splies just nodded all sour-faced. 'Gerron with it then, and stop wasting my bloody time.' And then he had another go at Clara the Clarion. 'I aren't telling you again, RentaGob. Bugger off up to your own end of the street.'

'I'll stay here as long as I wants to stay here, Hairpin,' she told him, and the next second he's got a long sword in his hand and he come hurtling out from the door like he was riding on a rocket. Yeah, honestly. He had a real sword!

He tried to swipe Clara across the knees with the sword and I could hear it whistling in the air it was moving so fast. He has to aim at the knees you see, because he can't reach any higher when he's moving fast or he'd lose his balance else. That's what Mrs Splies told me Mam anyway.

But I reckon Clara had been expecting him to try it on, because when he took a swipe she wasn't there. She was off up the street like she was riding on another rocket, only a sight faster one than Old Splies had got.

He was skreeking after her, 'If you comes down here again, RentaGob, I'll cut you in bits and roast you in me new gas cooker.'

Then he told Georgie Snood, 'Gerron with bloody fixing me cooker, Cod Face, and stop gawping at me like youm a bloody halfwit.' And he shook his sword under Georgie Snood's knees, and Georgie Snood went white. Yeah! He did! He went white! He was scared to death!

Mind you, I don't blame him. Because Old Splies was frothing at the mouth just like the Murtaghs' dog did when it went mad and bit the postman last Christmas. The postman had to go to hospital, you know. And he was in there for four months because they thought that he might go mad as well, and they had to be sure that he was going to be alright before they let him out again. Funny thing was, the postman was only out of the hospital for a week when he did go mad and had to be took to the Funny Farm. But everybody says that it's not the dog's fault. They says that the postman's missus is enough to drive anybody mad, so she's got the blame for it.

I've never seen Georgie Snood work so hard as he did to get that cooker fitted. And he never spoke a word all the time that we was in the house. I never said nothing neither, because Old Splies stood watching us every second, muttering under his breath and frothing at the mouth and swinging his sword, and it was going swish, swish, swish past our knees.

When we got out of the house George Snood told me, 'It's a good job for Old Splies that I'm a man who can control meself, Specs. He don't know how close he come to being knocked into the middle of next week. I nearly took that sword off him and shoved it up his arse, I'll tell you. It's a good job for him that I'm a man of iron self-control.'

To be honest, I was going to tell Georgie Snood to stop bullshitting me, because I knew that he'd been fritted to death of Old Splies. But then I remembered that I'd been fritted to death meself by that sword, so I didn't say nothing.

Then Georgie Snood said, 'Do you know what I think, Specs? I think that Old Splies is the one who's got plans to use that new cooker, and not his missus. Only it won't be to top himself, you know.'

No. I didn't know. I can't take it in. What he means, I mean.

And then he told me, 'Just you mark my words, Specs. I reckon that we shan't be seeing Mrs Splies again after she gets back from work tonight.'

Blimey! I thought. And I asked him. 'Does you mean that Old Splies is going to cut Mrs Splies up into little pieces and roast her in his new gas cooker?'

Georgie Snood winked and tried to look very wise. 'Eggzackly, Specs. Eggzackly!'

Now, this is the great mystery I told you about. Because the last couple of weeks Mrs Splies has been ever so happy at work, singing and smiling and whistling and she's had her hair permed as well. And last Saturday afternoon she was wearing a brand-new coat to go shopping in. But nobody down our street has seen hide nor hair of Old Splies ever since we fitted that new gas cooker.

I said to Mrs Masters that I wondered what had happened to Old Splies, and she laughed and told me, 'I reckon the wicked old sod's emigrated, Specs. Gone to a nice hot place. He should have gone there years ago.'

I can't help wondering about it, you

know. What's really happened to Old Splies, I mean. But I'll tell you one thing, I shan't be saying anything about it to anybody else apart from Mrs Masters. If he has gone it's good riddance to bad rubbish, aren't it. So I'll just do what everybody else in our street is doing, and mind me own business as far as what's happened to Old Splies.

Twenty-Four

I've been to the dance at the Memorial Hall tonight.

'Hot Dog Harry and his New Orleans Cool Cats' are the band. There's only three of them. Hot Dog Harry, Claudie Cloud and Reggie Allbutt. Hot Dog Harry is the crooner, Claudie Cloud plays the drums and Reggie Allbutt has got a trumpet, a clarinet, a trombone and a saxophone, and he keeps on switching over from one to the other, but it don't make much difference because he's hopeless on all of them. Hot Dog Harry works on the Co-op cheese counter down town, and he's never been to New Orleans in his life. In fact, he's never stepped foot outside the town except for a day trip to Weston-super-Mare one Easter. Neither have the other two, so I don't know where they get off calling themselves the New Orleans Cool Cats.

Johnny Merry asked him that once, and Hot Dog Harry looked all cool, rocking his head like a Big City Slicker, and told him, 'That's Show Biz, Kid. It's the way the cookie crumbles.'

On the poster outside the Hall, Hot Dog Harry calls himself 'England's Answer to Frank Sinatra'. He looks a bit like Frank Sinatra, small and skinny, but Hot Dog Harry hasn't got any hair so he wears a big black wig, and he's got a thin moustache like Errol Flynn's. When he's not crooning he plays the spoons. Yeah! Really! He's good as well. He runs them up both arms, down his legs and over his head. The trouble is when he runs them over his head all the Brylcreem comes off his wig onto the spoons and makes them stick together so he misses the beat. Reggie Allbutt goes mad when he does that because he says that it's unprofessional. It don't make any difference to Claudie Cloud though, he just goes on thumping the drums and clanging the cymbals ever so fast, and he keeps on jerking his head and shouting, 'Hey Bop a Ree Bop.'

He does that all the time, even when it's supposed to be a waltz or a Slow Foxtrot.

Tonight it was the Carnival Ball, and all the BigWigs were there at the Memorial Hall. All the Councillors and the Carnival Committee, and the Carnival Queen and her attendants. The way they was all acting you would have thought that they was real Royalty being gracious enough to come and mix with the rest of us, all the roughs and scruffs.

I wouldn't have bothered about that at all, only Glenda Shortway was one of the Carnival Queen's attendants, and she looked really smashing in her long dress and flowers in her hair. But she wouldn't even look at me. She sent a message across to Johnny Merry though, to tell him he could come and have a dance with her later on if he liked.

Johnny just acted like a real Big City Slicker. He told the girl who brought the message, 'Tell that Shortway Babe to cool it, because I ain't dancing tonight with any local yokels. All I'm going to do is to live fast, die young and have a good-looking corpse.'

I felt depressed after that. I just wish that sometimes girls would send me messages like they does to Johnny Merry to tell me that I could have a dance with them if I liked. I'd jump at the chance.

Then Hot Dog Harry made an announcement.

'Ladies and Gentlemen, tonight I have a wonderful surprise for you—'

'Have you given up singing then, Mr Sinatra?' Johnny Merry shouted, and all the roughs and scruffs cheered.

Hot Dog Harry looked daggers at us, then said real snotty, 'If there's any more interruptions from you lot, I shall call the police.'

All the roughs and scruffs cheered again.

Hot Dog Harry went all haughty, 'Ladies and Gentlemen, I have the honour to present Don Luis De Cordoba and his Lady wife, Dona Senora Carmencita De Cordoba, who have graciously consented to give a performance of the Argentinian Tango. I thank you.'

Hot Dog Harry bowed and all the respectable audience applauded. Then this bloke come on the floor wearing a mask so you couldn't see who he was, and one of those big Mexican hats and a short jacket with lots of sequins, and tight trousers. He'd got a massive backside and it wasn't half wobbling, and Johnny Merry shouted, 'Is that your arse, Pancho, or are you selling blancmanges?'

The bloke looked daggers at him, and then he sort of spun round and shouted, 'Venga, Carmencita. Venga.'

I don't know what that means, but I recognised the voice straight away. It was Idris Jones-Evans. His missus, Sybil, come running onto the floor then. She had a mask as well, and one of those long Spanish dresses on, and flowers behind her ears and she was waving a big fan around in the air.

Johnny Merry knew her straight away, and he shouted, 'The mask's not doing the job, Sybil, so keep the fan in front of your face for all our sakes.'

I had to laugh, but at the same time I felt a bit sorry for her. She can't help being so ugly, can she. But she's such a nasty cow, so I wasn't really all that much sorry for her.

'Ladies and Gentlemen, pray silence please, for "Tango de Noche",' Hot Dog

Harry shouted and told Claudie Cloud, 'Hit it, Cool Cat.'

Claudie Cloud's head jerked nearly off his shoulders and he shouted, 'Hey Bop a Ree Bop!' and started thumping the drums and clanging the cymbals like a madman, and Reggie Allbutt blew on his trumpet and Hot Dog Harry started crooning, 'My kind of town, Chicago is ...'

The trouble was none of them were in time with each other, and Idris and his missus kept on starting and stopping and starting and stopping, and I could see Sybil's face getting redder and redder, and all of a sudden Tommy TeeTee come in wearing his Salvation Army uniform with wellies, as drunk as a Bob Owler and playing his tambourine, singing 'Onward Christian Soldiers'.

Sybil chucked her fan at him like it was a spear, but he fell over and it went over him and landed straight in Hot Dog Harry's mouth just as he was reaching the high notes.

Hot Dog Harry started to choke, Sybil burst into tears and run out, and Idris went after her shouting, 'Que pasa, Carmencita? Que pasa, Querida?'

They had to take Hot Dog Harry to the

hospital because the fan was stuck in so deep nobody could pull it out, and they said the doctor would have to do it.

There was a bloke once in this town whose missus hit him while he was eating his dinner, and the fork he was eating with went right down his throat as well and got stuck there, and he had to have an operation. But you'd never believe what happened then. Somehow or other the operation altered his vocal chords and when he got better he could sing just like Frankie Laine.

He won the next Carnival Talent Competition, and then he won another Talent competition at Butlins, and now he's on the radio. He calls himself Tex La Rue now though, and never comes near the town. His missus is ever so sorry she hit him now, because he never comes near her neither.

Well, when they took Hot Dog Harry to the hospital there was a bit of a kerfuffle while the Carnival Committee was deciding what to do next, because without Hot Dog Harry they hadn't got a bandleader or a crooner, had they. Nor anybody who could play the spoons neither.

Then Sexy Rexy pushed himself forward, and all the roughs and scruffs started stamping their feet and cheering like mad.

You ought to see Sexy Rexy the Fighter Pilot. He's so oily you could pour him into a bottle and use him to run a car with. All the blokes uses Brylcreem but I reckon he's soaks his head in it every night, and he combs his hair dead flat and parts it in the middle and it shines and glitters like diamonds, and he's got one of them long moustaches that sticks out for miles each side of his head. He always wears a red and black striped blazer with brass buttons and a big badge on the pocket and white trousers and a bright blue silk shirt with a massive yellow cravat round his neck.

He keeps saying 'Wizard Prang!' all the time and he thinks that he's God's Gift to the women. He calls them all 'Poppet' when he's talking to them. But what I can't take in, is how all the women seems to love it when he comes to talk to them. They hangs about him like flies buzzing around a heap of horse muck.

He tells everybody that he was a Spitfire pilot in the war, and that he shot down over fifty Jerry planes. But Johnny Merry says that he knows a bloke who knew

Sexy Rexy in the war. The bloke told Johnny Merry that him and Sexy Rexy was in the Pay Corps together, and they both stayed in Llandudno all through the war, and the only Jerry they ever saw was working on a farm just outside the camp they was living on. The bloke said that they didn't even know he was a Jerry until the Victory in Europe Day party was being held and they saw the Jerry was cheering because the war was over and he could stop working on that farm and go back to being a hairdresser in Germany.

I'll tell you what though, Sexy Rexy didn't half give me a shock. He got on the stage and he borrowed Reggie Allbutt's trumpet and he started to play 'The Boogie Woogie Bugle Boy from Company C'. He couldn't half play that trumpet. I wish I could do something cool like that.

And then I had another shock. I saw Sophia come in. She was wearing a long white dress and her long black hair was hanging down over her shoulders, and she didn't half look beautiful. Me heart started to thump when I saw her looking at me, and I just lifted me hand and waved to her, and she waved back and smiled.

'Gooo onnnn!' Johnny Merry told me.

'Get in there. See if she'll have a dance with you.'

I plucked up all me courage and I walked across the floor towards her and me heart was thumping so hard that I couldn't get me breath.

But just as I got to her who should come walking in but Aubrey Jones-Evans. That lanky stuck-up prat! And she threw her arms round him and they went dancing off, and she never looked at me again all night.

I'll tell you something. I shan't half be glad when I'm in the Foreign Legion marching to Fort Zinderneuf ...

This Large Print Book for the partially sighted, who cannot read normal print, is published under the auspices of

THE ULVERSCROFT FOUNDATION

Other ...

THE ULVERSCROFT FOUNDATION

We hope that you have enjoyed this Large Print Book. Please think for a moment about those people who have worse eyesight problems than you . . . and are unable to even read or enjoy Large Print, without great difficulty.

You can help them by sending a donation, large or small to:

The Ulverscroft Foundation,
1, The Green, Bradgate Road,
Anstey, Leicestershire, LE7 7FU,
England.

or request a copy of our brochure for more details.

The Foundation will use all your help to assist those people who are handicapped by various sight problems and need special attention.

Thank you very much for your help.

Other MAGNA General Fiction Titles In Large Print

FRANCES ANNE BOND
Return Of The Swallow

JUDY GARDINER
All On A Summer's Day

IRIS GOWER
The Sins Of Eden

HELENE MANSFIELD
Some Women Dream

ELISABETH McNEILL
The Shanghai Emerald

ELIZABETH MURPHY
To Give And To Take

JUDITH SAXTON
This Royal Breed

Other MAGNA General Fiction Titles In Large Print

ELVI RHODES
Summer Promise

SALLY STEWART
The Women of Providence

ELISABETH McNEILL
Perseverance Place

NICHOLAS RHEA
Constable Among The Heather

JUDY TURNER
The Arcade

MISS READ
Village Affairs

PERFICK
The Darling Buds Of May